To: *The Lyon Family*

Scott glanced at the envelope addressed to the family. It should have gone to the executive offices, he thought as he walked away. Then the return address registered.

Judge Nicolette Bechet

He went back and picked up the letter. Nicki—with an address out of the city, in one of the rural parishes.

He fingered the envelope. Curious. A little excited, even.

He had as much right to open it as anyone. So without examining his logic too closely or too scrupulously, he slid a finger beneath the flap of the envelope.

Her signature was full of sweeps and flourishes—not what he would have expected at all.

Scott read the letter six times. She wanted to help the family find Margaret Hollander Lyon. Also, not what he would have expected.

Scott thought of all the dead-end leads that had been followed in the search for his aunt. Maybe he shouldn't burden the family until he knew more. He could talk to Nicki himself.

After all, he'd waited two years for the chance.

Dear Reader,

How important is family? And how profound are the
effects when there are rifts in the family? This final book in
THE LYON LEGACY, *Family Reunion,* explores the way two
people are affected by the difficulties in their families and
how their struggle to love one another leads to healing.

As I wrote about Scott Lyon and Nicki Bechet, I thought
of my own family and how easy it sometimes is to take
for granted the ties that bind us—ties of history, of shared
memories, of love. I also thought about the "families"
I've been blessed to find over the years—women friends,
neighbors, my sister writers in the romance community. All
of them are valuable, and I made a commitment, as I wrote,
to do more to nurture all those connections.

I hope as you read *Family Reunion,* you'll also think of
your family and be reminded how precious family is.

Happy reading.

Peg Sutherland

THE LYON LEGACY series from Harlequin Superromance:

The Lyon Legacy by Peg Sutherland, Roz Denny Fox and
    Ruth Jean Dale (Superromance 847)
Family Secrets by Ruth Jean Dale (Superromance 853)
Family Fortune by Roz Denny Fox (Superromance 859)
Family Reunion by Peg Sutherland (Superromance 865)

FAMILY REUNION
Peg Sutherland

HARLEQUIN®

TORONTO • NEW YORK • LONDON
AMSTERDAM • PARIS • SYDNEY • HAMBURG
STOCKHOLM • ATHENS • TOKYO • MILAN • MADRID
PRAGUE • WARSAW • BUDAPEST • AUCKLAND

ISBN 0-373-70865-3

FAMILY REUNION

Visit us at www.romance.net

Printed in U.S.A.

THE LYON FAMILY

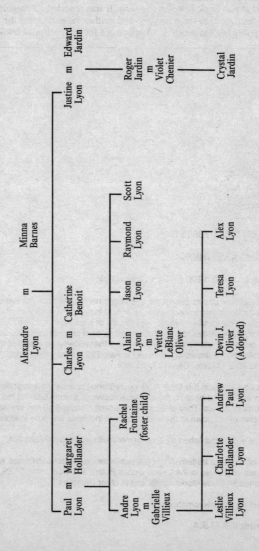

PROLOGUE

March 31, 1997

THE PACK OF about fifty reporters and camera-crew members outside the New Orleans court-house were hungry. That was how Scott Lyon would have described it. Hungry and circling for the kill.

Scott shifted the Minicam on his left shoulder. He glanced around, uncomfortable with the atmosphere. This felt personal and he knew why—Judge Nicolette Bechet.

Judge Bechet had handed down a controversial decision today in a child abuse case. The unsubstantiated allegations against a popular local politician had gripped the city's attention. Following as it did so closely on the judge's personal problems, which had also raised eyebrows and set tongues wagging, Judge Bechet's handling of the case—and the subsequent jail sentence she'd imposed—had drawn considerable scrutiny.

Now, the judge would be grilled, then roasted on tonight's late news and on the pages of the morning paper. Standard operating procedure. Nothing to get in an uproar over. Scott knew the drill.

But today, he had some qualms. Today, he kept remembering the haunted look in Judge Nicolette Bechet's eyes the last time he'd turned his camera on her.

Scott looked up at a second-story window in the sturdy old courthouse. The judge's office. He remembered its location from the first ambush interview, when he and WDIX-TV's ace, R. Bailey Ripken, had stormed the judge's chambers—just two days after her father had died of a drug overdose—and demanded answers to questions they'd had no business asking. The judge had been under siege ever since WDIX broke that story.

Scott regretted his part in exposing her family's secrets.

The horde of reporters was growing. Growing noisier and restless and more convinced of its right to know with every minute that passed.

Scott eased the camera off his shoulder. It was heavier than usual.

"What?"

That was R. Bailey Ripken. First name Ramona, a closely-guarded secret in journalistic circles; she'd confessed it to him her first week on the job. Scott inspired that kind of trust, especially from women.

"I need a pit stop," he said. It wasn't true. He didn't need to use a washroom. But something was driving him to get out of this mob, something he couldn't explain to himself, much less to the Crescent City's exposé queen.

"Now? You've got to be kidding? She's bound to come out any minute!"

"I won't be long."

"Scott!"

He was already elbowing his way through the crowd, and was tempted to ditch the pricey camera. He'd heard the disbelief in Bailey's voice. But what could she do? Have him fired? He smiled grimly to himself. Okay, so sometimes family connections gave a guy the edge.

He'd been around long enough to know better than to march right up to the front door. He'd have the entire gang of reporters right behind him. He went to a side door. He was familiar with the building layout. As he mounted the broad stairs to the second floor, his sneakers squeaking on the well-worn marble, his heart was thumping a little harder than usual. He knew the rules and what he had in mind broke most of them.

Maybe even having the name Lyon on his media credentials wouldn't save his rear end if this got out.

To hell with it.

He made his way through the little maze of hallways to the judges' offices. Room 201. A dark oak door, seven-feet high and imposing. Scott realized his fingers were cramping around his camera, he was gripping it that tightly.

What was going on with him, that he was reacting this way, sabotaging his own work? Was this the first sign of burnout? Boredom? Just plain disgust? Or was it, after all, as simple as one man's instinctive urge to come to the rescue of a woman he wanted to impress?

He opened the door without knocking, slipped in and closed it behind him.

Judge Nicolette Bechet didn't even seem startled. From her desk, her keen blue eyes zeroed in on his camera and froze. "Leave. Now."

She was known for her clipped, no-frills style in court. She intimidated a lot of people that way. Scott wasn't intimidated—he knew the technique. His Aunt Margaret used it well.

"Look out your window."

She took a breath, her nostrils flaring almost imperceptibly. "You've overstepped your bounds, Mr. Lyon."

She knew his name. He doubted if his family connections bought him much with her.

"I know. Now look out the window, Judge Bechet."

She remained rigid, her gaze unflinching. A distinctive cleft marked her pointed chin, adding an aura of strength to her face. Her hair was the color of honey, streaked by the sun and pulled back loosely from her narrow face.

Nicolette Bechet wasn't beautiful, but Scott hadn't been able to get her off his mind since he'd videotaped her interview with Bailey. Despite her cool, she hadn't been able to completely hide the haunted look in her wide blue eyes. It wasn't just the look of a grieving daughter, he'd decided. It went deeper than that.

The probing questions she'd refused to answer during the interview—or in the ten days since, when every reporter in New Orleans had quizzed her over and over—had confirmed Scott's guess. Judge Bechet had unfinished business in her family. Old business.

"I could very easily have you removed," she

said now with steely control. She spoke precisely, with no hint of her Cajun roots.

"But who'll remove *them?*" he asked.

For the first time she seemed to see him as a human being and not merely a video camera on two legs. Her eyes met his, first challenging, then showing just a little uncertainty. Scott again registered the thud of his heartbeat and knew better than to attribute it solely to the fact that he was betraying his colleagues by warning Nicolette Bechet about the media attack awaiting her. No, it was more than that. The judge got under his skin.

"Them?"

He nodded at the window.

She stood slowly. She still wore her robe, open over a dove-gray silk blouse buttoned securely to a little stand-up collar. Gray cuffs showed. Her skirt was black and as she moved from behind her desk in the direction of the window, he saw that it fell a very proper two inches below her knees. Her calves were shapely, even in her no-nonsense flat-heeled shoes. Trim ankles.

But it was her eyes that made his mouth go dry.

A startling shade of blue and completely unrelenting, they weren't the windows to any soul he could see, except in those brief moments when she was caught unaware.

She looked out the window, then stiffened. ''I see.'' She looked back at him. ''And you're here because…?''

''I didn't think you'd want to be ambushed.''

She made a cynical smile. ''And in return…''

He didn't blame her. He was a television-news cameraman, after all.

''The back exit is clear,'' he said. ''You can make it to your car that way without running into trouble.''

She studied him. Then very carefully she took off her robe, folded it and draped it over the back of her leather chair. She replaced it with a suit jacket, picked up a briefcase and started for the door. He stood to one side.

''This doesn't get you anything,'' she said. ''Not the inside scoop. Not an exclusive. Nothing.''

Her upper lip was delicate and perfectly formed. Her lower lip was full and soft. She didn't have the look of a woman who wasted time being kissed.

''I don't expect anything,'' he said gruffly.

She didn't challenge his claim, but her eyes remained filled with skepticism.

She marched down the hall. He wanted to follow her, but couldn't justify doing so. She didn't want his protection, and he had no business offering it.

He returned to the pack of reporters and waited with them until someone got word that Judge Nicolette Bechet had given them all the slip. Scott tried not to smile as R. Bailey Ripken contributed to the rash of frustrated profanities that rippled through the throng of reporters. There would be no story tonight.

The next day, however, was a different matter. At a late-afternoon press conference, it was announced that Judge Nicolette Bechet had resigned her post. She wasn't available for questioning.

Her apartment had been vacated.

CHAPTER ONE

Bayou Sans Fin, November 1999

"SILENCE! NOW!"

The cranky cockatiel's command merely added to the usual morning chaos around the breakfast table at Cachette en Bayou Farm.

Tony and his cousin Toni were perfecting a riff in the song the two were writing for their zydeco band. Beau's baby girl was demanding attention using the best technique known to six-month-olds. Milo the mutt whined for a biscuit; Michel's current live-in girlfriend whined about her hair. And twelve-year-old Jimmy was practicing his forward pass over everyone's head, using the six unsuspecting cats as target.

Nicki sighed.

"Quiet!" That was Perdu the cockatiel again, more frantic this time. He made an impatient little skip on Maman Riva's shoulder. The histrionics, Nicki knew, would serve no good purpose.

The Bechet family was a freight train with no brakes.

"We start electrical work this week," Nicki announced quietly, spooning up a slice of pink grapefruit.

"This one's a bullet!" Jimmy shrieked. "Watch your noggins."

Jimmy had not been raised to throw footballs at the breakfast table. This Nicki knew. His side of the family was normal, sane, well behaved. But as soon as they reached Cachette en Bayou, some sort of insanity gene kicked in and they were off and running.

Nicki swallowed the bite of grapefruit. "That means we'll be without lights. Without refrigerator. Without hot water. Without air-conditioning." Nobody took any notice of her. She thought wryly of her days on the bench. People had sat up and taken notice when Judge Nicolette Bechet spoke. Those days were gone forever. "It could go on for a week or more."

Still no reaction. Yet Nicki knew that each and every one of them would look at her after several hours without power and demand to know how she could have sprung this on them without warning.

"This I cannot believe!" Maman Riva said,

shaking her head and brushing Perdu's beak with the fluff of snow-white curls peeking from beneath her purple paisley turban. "Months she is missing and not a word. Outrageous! Scandalous!"

"Shut up!" Perdu demanded, his tone even more strident.

Riva Reynard Bechet waved her cotton napkin in the cockatiel's face. "Where you learn to talk to your elders that way, you so-and-so? *You* shut up, you hear?" She surreptitiously dropped a warm biscuit in the vicinity of Milo's tan-and-gray nose. "You get old, nobody pays you no mind. This is the problem. My problem. Her problem. I try to keep my family in line, nobody pays me mind. She disappears, nobody pays her no mind."

Riva was still obsessing over the disappearance of Margaret Lyon, the revered matriarch of the Lyons of New Orleans. Every morning since the story had broken in the *Times-Picayune* a month ago, Riva couldn't wait to read the latest details. The Lyons seemed to hold some kind of special fascination for her, as if they were royalty.

The Lyons themselves certainly seemed to think so, Nicki thought. But it annoyed her that her own grandmother should have such skewed thinking. Didn't she remember it was the Lyons and their TV station that had smeared the Bechet name, ruined her career?

Riva may have forgotten, but Nicki definitely had not.

"Perhaps you should stay in town with James and Cheryl while we do the electrical work, Maman," Nicki said, instead of what she was thinking.

"You're wanting, I think, to run me off my farm." Riva didn't look up from the newspaper. "See here, now, those Lyon scoundrels file junk in the court. They try to steal her TV station. Lord-a-mercy, is a great lot of peril in growing old."

Junk in the court. Nicki supposed her grandmother meant an injunction of some kind. When it suited her, Riva could be so Cajun she was almost unintelligible to the rest of the world. Riva was sharp, had always run the Bechet family like a benign dictator. Papa Linc Bechet had been no match for her. Even Riva's two surviving children, Nicki's aunt Simone and uncle James, couldn't get her to budge once she'd made up her mind. They kept trying to persuade her to move into town, sell the old farm or, better yet, let them run it.

That was usually when Riva lapsed into dialect and stared at them as if she'd never heard a word of proper English in her life.

The same way she'd been acting for the past six months whenever Nicki tried to have a reasonable conversation with her grandmother about Cachette en Bayou Farm. Riva didn't want to fix up the farmhouse, which was crumbling around the edges. She didn't want to sell. She just wanted things to be the way they'd always been. At least that was what Nicki concluded. Maman would not discuss it, so it was virtually impossible to know with any certainty what the eighty-four-year-old woman's motives were.

"We need to talk about the house, Maman. It's not going to be habitable for the next week. You should—"

A football landed in the huge pottery bowl of cheese grits. Gasps and giggles and groans broke out, along with howls of outrage aimed at the skinny twelve-year-old future pro quarterback, who should have been in school in the city.

"Why you not in school?" Beau demanded.

"They probably don't want him around, either," Tony said.

"Now you leave my Jimmy boy alone." Riva waved off the comments. "Come here, Jimbo. Give an old lady a thrill."

The sheepish adolescent gave her a hug. Nicki supposed her youngest cousin was currently in residence at the farm because his mother was having another of her famous migraines. Nicki suspected what incapacitated her uncle James's society wife had more to do with bourbon than migraines, but she certainly wasn't about to say so. Nor would anyone else in the family.

Then again, the Bechet family was enough to produce a headache, that much she could vouch for.

"Maman—" Nicki made another attempt "—if you stay with James for the next week, you can help out until Cheryl gets back on her feet, Jimmy wouldn't miss any school and—"

"You must find Mrs. Lyon."

Nicki tried not to grind her molars. "Maman, the Lyons do not need my help finding anyone."

"Oh, but yes. I am thinking they do."

"Besides which, I am not remotely interested in helping the Lyon family." The volunteer work Nicki did was dear to her heart. She did searches for people, usually on behalf of adopted children looking for their birth parents. She did it because she knew from personal experience what it felt like to be abandoned.

She did not do it for millionaire families whose toughest decisions centered around whose life to ruin next.

Riva folded the newspaper neatly and clasped her hands on top of it. "Good. This is decided."

"No, it's not decided!"

Nicki realized from the silence following her words that she must have raised her voice. Raising one's voice to Maman Riva was not recommended. Nicki strove to sound reasonable.

"Maman, I have work to do. Renovation work here at the farm—"

Riva shook her head. "Not necessary."

"It is unless you want the place to fall in on top of you."

Riva looked around, seemed to consider that possibility. "The boys have their cabin. Simone, she and John are settled. James and Cheryl, they have a big fancy house." Riva shrugged. "You, you might find a nice man yourself if you had noplace to go. Me, I am old. If it falls on my head, I go on to heaven. Better than this mean old world, where old women disappear and not a body cares." She reached over, patted Nicki's hand and smiled the smile no one could resist.

"You help find Margaret Lyon, that's a good girl."

"They haven't asked for my help."

"So you go to them."

Nicki stared at her grandmother. Riva seemed to have forgotten just who had caused all the upheaval in the Bechet family two years earlier. Nicki would be just as happy if this morning's headline reported that the entire Lyon family had been sentenced straight to hell with no chance for parole. But she couldn't say that to her grandmother.

"I have too many search projects already. I—"

"You do good jobs for people," Riva interrupted, still smiling. "You will do a good job for the Lyons."

Nicki heard the rattle and chug of the pickup truck belonging to the couple helping with renovations. She stood. "This discussion is over. I have work to do."

Riva stood and began collecting empty plates. "You call the Lyons. Make your grandmother happy."

Nicki was accustomed to the fact her grandmother never played fair. Well, let her think she'd won. Nicki had real work to do.

SCOTT LYON LEANED against the wall closest to the conference-room door, one foot propped on an empty chair, his arms crossed tightly over his chest.

He ought to resign from the station.

Hell, he ought to resign from the family.

The morning editorial meetings at WDIX-TV were wearing him down. These days the time was rarely spent assigning stories and scheduling tapings, as it should be. Instead, the meetings disintegrated into bickering as everyone jockeyed for control. He should be used to it by now; it had been this way in the Lyon family all his life. He'd been weaned on his father's bellyaching that he'd been robbed of his inheritance, a victim of greed and unfairness. Now, thanks to Aunt Margaret's disappearance and the injunction filed by Scott's three older brothers—Jason, Raymond and Alain—the ugliness simmering beneath the surface for as long as Scott could remember had exploded to the surface.

Jason, the sales manager at the station, had obviously made it to the conference room first this morning. He occupied the chair at the head of the table, a seat usually reserved for the news director. But the news director wasn't family. To hear

Jason and Alain tell it, even family wasn't family these days.

"We don't need to be covering that," Jason said now about a press conference for a beleaguered city official whose career was drowning in scandal.

The city official was a buddy of Alain, the oldest of the four brothers. Scott pursed his lips to keep from opening his mouth. He didn't get involved in decisions made by his brothers. He preferred the role of neutral bystander. He pretended not to register the news director's rolling eyes.

"It's news," Bailey Ripken said with ill-disguised contempt. "That's what we do, Jason. Cover news."

"Are we a tabloid scandal sheet now?" Jason Lyon looked around the table at the assignment editors and reporters who had managed to get the news on the air for years without his assistance or input. "Is that what we're stooping to? Airing people's dirty linen? I don't think so. Lyon Broadcasting stands for more than that. Next story."

Scott slipped out the door and closed it behind him as the words "journalistic integrity" and "muckraking" filled the air in the tense little conference room.

He stood in the corridor for a minute, working his jaw muscles and battling the urge to walk straight out the front door. He could dig ditches, for God's sake. Drive a cab. He didn't have to put up with this.

When he was calm enough to face the world without spitting out some kind of venom he would later regret, Scott made his way to the break room. He inserted quarters into the vending machine and treated himself to a breakfast of hot sweet coffee and two somewhat stale sweet rolls. He wolfed them down, barely noticing the taste.

His coffee had just gotten cool enough to drink when his cousin André walked into the break room. The hum of conversation quieted with the presence of the station's embattled general manager.

André Lyon looked embattled, all right. At fifty-eight, he had always been tall and square-shouldered. But Scott thought his cousin's shoulders had begun to sag with the weight of all that had happened since the station's fiftieth anniversary this past summer. First, André's father and co-founder of WDIX-TV, Paul Lyon, had died. Then, the day of the funeral, André's mother had vanished. Most everyone had assumed that Margaret Lyon simply needed to get away from the glare of publicity, find a quiet spot to grieve and let go of the man with whom she'd shared her life and founded a broadcasting dynasty.

Then signs began to point to the possibility of foul play.

And in the midst of absorbing that emotional blow, the family had received another: Jason, Raymond and Alain were challenging Paul Lyon's will in court. André wasn't the rightful heir, they claimed. He wasn't a Lyon and they swore they had the documentation to prove it.

Scott was incredulous, and ashamed that his own brothers would pull such a disgusting stunt. The rest of the family was equally stunned. And André, it appeared to Scott, had been nearly broken by the series of events.

Breathing out a heavy sigh, Scott took his litter to the trash bin beside the machines. André looked up as he passed. His once decisive and calm face looked distracted.

"Oh, Scott. How goes it? News conference already over?"

Rising to the occasion, trying to sound normal. Scott had to respect that in his cousin. It was one of the things he'd always admired in Aunt Margaret, too. His own side of the Lyon family should take a lesson.

"I slipped out," he said, hoping André wouldn't ask why.

André nodded, reached out and punched a button on the coffee machine. A cup dropped into the slot, and coffee began to trickle.

"Any word?" Scott asked, knowing no further explanation was necessary.

André shook his head. "I'm afraid not. Unless…" Retrieving the cup from the machine, he shook his head again.

They walked out of the break room together.

"Unless what?"

André took a deep swallow of his coffee and grimaced. "Unless you count the crackpots. A lot of crackpots. Gaby and I have waded through more crank calls and useless leads since the story broke." He paused and gave his cousin a poor imitation of an encouraging smile. "We're tired, that's all."

"If I can help…" Scott almost hated to make the perfunctory offer. He doubted that help from his branch of the family tree would be welcome.

André put a hand on his shoulder. "I appreciate that, Scott. I know you're in an awkward position here."

"No. I stay out of it. And I mean what I say. If I can help, I want to. Aunt Margaret…" His throat grew unexpectedly tight at the mention of her name. He could almost see the grande dame of the Lyon family marching purposefully down a corridor at Lyon Broadcasting in one of her severe navy dresses, head high, shoulders back. Being seventy-seven hadn't slowed her down a bit. "I think a lot of her."

That was an understatement. Scott wondered if André knew that. The truth was, he loved Margaret Hollander Lyon; she'd been more of a mother to him than his own mother, and more of a role model for him than his own weak-willed father. As the youngest child in the family, almost a tagalong, born as his parents' marriage was disintegrating into cold silence and emotional withdrawal, if not divorce, Scott had found little stability or warmth in his life. Until he got to know Aunt Margaret.

"I appreciate that, Scott. But the truth is, I don't know that there's much any of us can do. Except wait and pray."

"I'm not much good at either of those," Scott admitted.

"Me, neither. And I hate like the devil having to learn it under these circumstances."

As André went his way, Scott turned in the direction of the newsroom—in time to see Raymond and Jason lurking in the door outside Raymond's office in the accounting department. The morning news conference obviously over, they apparently had been watching Scott's conversation with André. Feeling the building closing in around him, Scott wheeled into the newsroom without acknowledging his brothers.

In the newsroom a handful of reporters and camera technicians were beginning to gather. Early mornings were the slowest time of the day at WDIX-TV. Reporters and crew members straggled in and milled around waiting for their coffee to kick in. Sometime before noon, the activity cranked up. Phones rang, voices called out across the room, and chaos ruled. By late afternoon the chaos was organized and transformed into the evening news.

Scott could remember a time when he'd been excited by the process. When the desire to be the first to crack a story had been in his blood. But it didn't seem to be there now.

All he felt these days, after years of watching competition and greed consume his family, was the desire to be someplace else.

He wondered, sometimes, if that was what had happened to Aunt Margaret.

"Hey, Scott," said the sweet, beguiling voice

of the newsroom clerk behind him, "what's shakin'?"

He turned to give her a smile. Tiffany Marie Dalcour was young, just out of college, and ambitious. She seemed to think that cultivating the only single male Lyon in the building might somehow further her goal of making it on-camera herself.

"Not much, Tiffany."

She was sorting mail for the newsroom. Piles and piles of mail. She didn't miss a beat even as she intensified her smile at Scott. "So there'll be no broadcast tonight, then?"

He laughed, and she looked pleased. At thirty-four, he had no interest whatsoever in the twenty-four-year-old, but he returned her teasing, anyway. "We'll make it up if we have to."

"Oops," she said, tossing an envelope aside. "That one should have gone to the executive offices, I guess."

Scott glanced down at the envelope. It was addressed to "The Lyon Family." He started to walk away when the name on the return address registered.

Nicolette Bechet.

He went back and picked up the envelope. Nicolette Bechet, with an address out of the city, in one of the rural districts.

He fingered the envelope. He was curious. A little excited, even.

The Lyon Family.

He had as much right to open it as anyone.

Without examining his logic too scrupulously, he slid a finger beneath the flap of the envelope.

Her signature was full of sweeps and flourishes, not what he would have expected at all.

And she wanted to help the family find Margaret Lyon. Also not what he would have expected.

He read the letter six times. Finding people was a hobby of hers, the letter said. The letter recounted some of her successes. Scott was impressed. Intrigued. He thought about the weary tone of André's voice when he'd spoken of all the dead-end leads he and his wife had followed up on. No need to add to the burden, Scott told himself.

He could talk to the former judge himself.

After all, he'd been wanting to for two years.

CHAPTER TWO

SCOTT WAS A CITY BOY. He knew very little about Louisiana's fabled bayou country. Recreation in Scott's mind was a late night in the French Quarter following his nose to exotic new cuisine or his ears to the hottest new jazz or blues musicians.

He'd heard of Bayou Sans Fin. Some kind of family connection, although he couldn't think what.

Bayou Sans Fin—bayou without end. The idea sent a little shiver along the back of his neck as he steered his low-slung two-seater along the snaking blacktop. Live oaks met overhead, blocking out the sky and the sun, dripping gray Spanish moss to within inches of his New Orleans Saints ball cap. Dense thickets of cypress, hackberry and willow trees fronted the marshes and swamps, which were neither land nor water, but some mysterious in-between territory that exuded an aura of danger.

The only sign of human habitation was the occasional mailbox. Narrow dirt driveways were overgrown with vines and weeds and other plant life alien to someone who'd grown up around the Garden District's immaculately sculptured flower beds. The driveways, he supposed, signaled the possibility of homes. Of people. The kind of people who wanted to live far beyond the reach of prying eyes and friendly voices, perhaps.

Mostly, however, Scott imagined other life forms. Gators and muskrats and mink lurked in the dense overgrowth, maybe keeping a wary eye on the sleek red monster Scott drove. He imagined he could feel their wild unfathomable eyes on him and shivered again.

Then again, maybe it wasn't gator eyes he imagined at all. Maybe the eyes he conjured up in his imagination were equally unfathomable, but as blue as the bits and pieces of sky visible through the canopy of trees.

He was going to see her. After two years, the memory of her had never quite vanished, and now he was going to talk to her. Get to know her maybe. Find out about the finely drawn upper lip that didn't quite match the lush lower lip.

His mind was out of control.

He was supposed to be at work, lugging a

video camera all over the Crescent City. Point, pan, zoom. Hours of taping for minutes of on-air time, measuring yours against theirs, holding your breath to see which reporter nailed the lead story that day, strutting if you won, clamping your jaw and saying wait till tomorrow if you ended up on the cutting-room floor.

He crossed a rickety plank bridge, holding his breath all the way, then spotted an enormous mailbox on the left a few yards ahead. It bore the name Bechet, hand-lettered in yellow on red. His tires squealed a protest as he wheeled into the turn and hit dirt and rock. A tree limb brushed the shiny paint on the passenger door; vines hung low above his open car. He wondered what he'd do if a snake dropped out of the trees overhead.

About two hundred yards off the highway, the driveway cleared and widened marginally, revealing a cypress archway with a sign—Welcome to Cachette en Bayou Farm. Hideaway on the Bayou. The sign might give lip service to the idea of welcome, but Scott wouldn't have called the entrance inviting by any stretch of the imagination. He braked almost to a halt.

Unbidden came the image of the massive iron fence encircling Lyoncrest, the impressive family mansion in the Garden District. With its sleek bronze lions posing at the front gate, Lyoncrest had sometimes struck him as uninviting—as this dark entrance seemed to him now.

He glanced up at the letter from Nicolette Bechet clipped to the visor. He had, after all, been invited. Well, not him specifically. But a representative of the Lyon family. Which he was. So he wasn't intruding. He drove on.

The house came into view. He didn't know what he'd expected, but this wasn't it. The building wandered in every direction, turning here, rising there, making another twist just when you expected it to finally come to a stop. Obviously it had been added to over the years—perhaps every time a new generation of Bechets was born.

What appeared to be the original core of the house was a square three-story structure made of unevenly formed bricks the color of just-boiled shrimp. The house rose on stilts above the unkempt yard, the ground level ringed with small windows, letting scant light into what was likely an above-ground cellar. Wide, steep steps rose to the second-floor gallery and main entrance, which was unimposing and standing wide open. Shuttered windows were as high as any door. Wings went off in both directions, one of natural cypress, one painted a dreary dun color. The roof was tin, the shutters hung crookedly, and the chimney was a listing steeple of bricks that appeared ready to topple and inflict serious bodily harm.

The ungainly house was surrounded by pickup trucks—Scott counted six—in varying states of repair, and one finned Cadillac circa 1960. The house leaked noise from every open door and window—sawing and hammering and drilling and conflicting music, zydeco from the cypress wing and country from the other.

This surely could not be the home of Nicolette Bechet.

He pulled his sports car in beside a polished blue pickup with fancy stripes, farthest from the disaster-waiting-to-happen chimney, and questioned his presence here one last time before he killed the engine.

Then he saw her.

She was hanging out a third-story window, precariously braced with one boot-clad foot inside the window, the other on the tin roof. She was tugging on one of the dilapidated shutters. A claw hammer hung from a loop on the overalls she wore. A white painter's cap with its brim yanked to one side covered her head, but didn't come close to covering her hair, which had been sleek and gold the last time he'd seen her. Now, it was long and wild and spilling to her shoulder blades.

If Scott's heart hadn't lurched in his chest and his breath come out in a whoosh when he saw her, he'd never have believed that figure was the carefully buttoned-up judge he remembered.

He took the keys out of the ignition, removed the letter from the visor clip, opened the car door and got out, never taking his eyes off her.

She almost lost her balance when the shutter pulled free. With a fierce grunt, she turned and shoved it off the edge of the steep roof, calling after it as it rattled and fell and splintered on the ground, ''Now you're trash. Irritating trash at that.''

He looked up at her, his reaction not diminishing. Her eyes landed on him. ''Who are you?''

She'd certainly lost her judicial manner in two years. He grinned.

''Scott Lyon.'' He fluttered the letter in the air by way of explanation.

She hoisted her other foot out of the window and stood on the roof, hands on hips, feet apart. ''Get the hell off my farm.''

She must've misunderstood. His grin deepened. ''I got your letter.''

"And I've got a shotgun I can put my hands on in forty-five seconds flat if I don't see your rear end headed in that direction by the time I get back inside."

She gave that a second to sink in, her expression granite, then turned and crawled back in the window, more graceful than anything he'd ever before seen in overalls and cowboy boots.

"Best leave," came a voice from the zydeco side of the house. Scott looked into the amused eyes of a dark bearded man with a big smile and an industrial-strength drill dangling lightly from one beefy hand. "She don't be a half-bad hand with a shotgun."

Scott was still grinning. "She sent for me."

The workman shook his head. "She'll send you to hell in a quick minute, that's what."

A shot rang out. Scott flinched. He glanced up at the window. She stood there with the shotgun pointed skyward, glaring.

"Warning shot," the workman explained. "Me, I don't mess with her."

"She's worth the effort, seems to me."

"We fancy our hides."

"Maybe I fancy hers."

The slash of white teeth against black beard

grew wider. "I understand that, you bet. Still, I'd duck under the gallery if I was you."

Scott looked up. She seemed to be taking aim. "Good idea."

He bounded up the steep steps, all new boards, raw and unfinished but sturdy, a match for the new planks on the porch. A mutt dozed in a circle of dappled sunlight and raised two sleepy eyes to take him in. The animal was less wary of visitors, apparently, than the lady of the house. Scott peered through the open front door. The rooms were dark. The foyer was broad, rising two stories. He stepped in.

"I heard the shooting. I'm guessing you've already seen my granddaughter."

He turned to the left, where an old woman sat in a straight-backed rocker beside a fireplace in a rustic parlor. No arches and fancy work here, just a square serviceable room with scarred hardwood floors and plaster walls that were gutted at intervals to reveal electrical wiring.

"I'm Scott Lyon," he said, taking off his ball cap. "I think she's forgotten. She wrote me. The family, actually."

A cat was curled up in the old woman's lap and an imposing white bird with brilliant orange markings sat on her narrow shoulder. "Scott. I don't know a Scott."

"Prescott Lyon, ma'am. Charles Lyon's youngest son." Scott was used to people not knowing him but recognizing his family name.

"You may call me Riva, Prescott."

"Pleased to meet you, ma'am."

"You may not call me ma'am. Understood?"

"Yes, ma'am."

She gave him a hard look, a look he'd already seen once today from the woman on the roof.

"Yes, Riva."

She nodded slightly. "Better. So, you the son of Charles Lyon. The ne'er-do-well, yes?"

Her outspokenness reminded him of Aunt Margaret and made him instantly at ease with her, even though she couldn't have been more different from his aunt on the surface. Riva looked much older, what with her face so lined and weathered and the slumped way she sat in her rocker. Yes, far less vigorous than Margaret Lyon. Also, Margaret wore impeccable navy suits and dresses, decorating herself with nothing more elaborate than a single strand of pearls. In contrast, Riva wore a garish purple wrap of some kind, a red-and-yellow scarf, gaudy jewelry dripping from her ears and her neck and her wrists, and ballet slippers on her tiny feet.

"Yes," he said, liking the woman well enough not to take offense at her assessment of his father. "There are those who might describe my father as a ne'er-do-well."

She cackled. "Never mind. They called me worse."

"Uh-oh," said the bird.

Riva glanced over Scott's shoulder and her face broke into a smile. "Ah, Nicki. Your guest has arrived."

Scott turned slightly to take her in. With her this close, he could almost feel the animosity rising off her in waves. It made his heartbeat accelerate.

She had left the shotgun upstairs.

He extended a hand, gave her a warm smile. "Thanks for not shooting me."

She ignored his hand. "I asked you to leave."

"Actually you *told* me to leave."

"Nicki, *m'enfant,* how rude. This young man, he will think the bayou makes us inhospitable."

Nicki glared at the old woman. "You stay out of this."

The bird joined in with a shrill "Shut up!"

"You taught him to speak, I take it," Scott said to Nicki.

Riva cackled. He thought he heard approval.

"I'm only here to take you up on your offer," he said, tapping the folded letter against his palm. "I suppose I should've called first, but—"

"I have no idea what you're talking about."

Her blue eyes flashed and her wavy hair almost quivered with emotion.

He gave her the letter. She opened it and read it as if she'd never seen it before. Then she balled it up and threw it into the open fireplace.

"Maman, you go too far," she said, her voice lapsing into a Cajun cadence he hadn't heard her use before. She looked at Scott. "I'm sorry you wasted your time. My grandmother is toying with us, and I apologize for her, since I doubt she'll apologize for herself. Now if you'll excuse me, I have work to do."

"But…"

She was leaving. Walking away. He took a step in her direction, but didn't know what to say to change her mind or to pull her into the emotional whirlwind she always created in him.

Maybe if he simply followed and kissed her.

"Wouldn't do that," Riva said.

He spun around. "Wouldn't do what?"

Riva laughed and didn't answer. "Sit," she said, and gestured at a matching rocker, occupied at the moment by a ball of yellow-and-gray fur, which proved to be two sleeping cats. When he approached, one hissed while leaping off the chair, the other stood on the armrest and waited patiently for him to sit. Then the feline dropped into his lap and circled four times before settling.

"She likes you, my cat."

"Your granddaughter does not."

"My cat is a better judge of people."

"I'd like to think so." He waited.

"It is true, what the letter says. Nicki finds people. She uses computers."

"She doesn't seem inclined to help."

Riva shrugged. "She hates the Lyons."

He didn't have to ask why. "Then why am I here?"

"Because you want to find Margaret."

He ran his hand over the cat's fur and studied Riva Bechet. He had the most compelling sense that he was also here because Riva Bechet wanted to find Margaret, as well.

NICKI TOOK HER FURY to the pier, the only structure on the entire 106 acres that wasn't falling apart. She looked at the film of green duckweed covering the still water and fumed.

How dare she!

Her grandmother was an unrepentant busybody. Among her many flaws, that was one nobody disputed. Riva Reynard Bechet believed she knew how everyone's life should be managed, and she never hesitated to jump in and try.

But this! Inviting the Lyons to Cachette en Bayou and using Nicki's name to do it.

When she turned back toward the house, a gasp of outrage escaped her lips. Riva had brought him onto the brick patio. He was holding a chair for her. Riva placed a hand on his arm as she lowered herself into the chair. She was smiling up at him. He was smiling back.

Nicki wheeled around to face the water again. She couldn't stand this.

"Hey, Quick-Nick, what's she done now?"

Nicki squeezed her eyes shut at the sound of her eighteen-year-old cousin Toni's voice. Not now, she pleaded with whoever had the power to intervene in her life. She felt the slight give of the boards as the girl dropped onto the pier.

"I was out at the cabin and heard the gunshot. Who is he?"

Nicki drew a deep breath and opened her eyes.

The water was still smooth and green. Elephant ears still swayed in the barest of breezes, and clumps of bulrush still provided nesting areas for black-crowned night heron and red-tailed hawks. A smattering of low-lying fog clung to the opposite shore. You could count on the bayou, from moment to moment, from year to year. The only change from seconds earlier was a snowy egret that had dropped silently onto a cypress log lodged against the opposite bank. The bird was graceful and still, unlike anything in Nicki's life.

"I'm coming back as an egret in my next life," she said.

Toni chuckled. "Not me. I'm going to be a gator. Snap at anything that makes me see red. Course, I guess you've got that covered this go round."

A wry grin touched Nicki's lips. "Smart mouth."

"Yeah, but I've got my bad points, too."

The egret took to the air, again without a sound.

"He's a Lyon," Nicki said. "Scott Lyon."

"A Lyon? Oh, the big shots in the news. Some old lady ran off with the family fortune or something. Right?"

Nicki had a moment of envy for the oblivi-

ousness that could still be one's companion at
eighteen. The world remained narrowed to one's
immediate concerns—a boy who looked good in
his jeans, a weekend gig for the band you believed was your heart and soul, the certainty that
you'd always be a size six no matter how many
cheeseburgers you ate.

"Something like that."

"You gonna find her?"

"No."

"His brains you were blowing out, then?"

"Yeah."

"Why? He looks cute enough from here."

Nicki restrained herself from looking. She
didn't have to. She could will Scott Lyon into
her mind's eye with a minimum of effort. He had
changed since that day two years ago. His hair
was short now, clipped so close to his head you
couldn't grab a handful. And it was mostly silver,
even though he had to be about her age, which
was thirty-four. He wore a tiny gold hoop in his
left ear, the perfect size to hug his earlobe and
no more. Strong bones formed his face, giving
him a chiseled jaw and a square chin, high cheek-
bones and the nose from a statue by Michelan-
gelo. His taut face was tanned to perfect gold, his
eyes a smoky gray.

Those eyes had haunted her for two years.

She had been inclined to trust them two years ago when he'd burst into her chambers. Nicki usually trusted her instincts about people, and her instincts had told her Scott Lyon had no hidden agenda. He said he'd come to help her and he meant just that.

Silly her.

"I don't like the Lyons," she said.

"Because they run the TV station that started all that stuff after Uncle David died of a drug overdose?"

So maybe teenagers weren't completely oblivious. Nicki felt the strongest urge to stalk away. But she did that a lot. So this time she stayed put.

"That's right."

"Dad said it was all true."

Nicki opened her mouth to say that Toni's father was a straitlaced coldhearted son of a you-know-what, but she caught herself. Uncle James might indeed be a little chilly where emotions were concerned, but he was still Toni's father. Besides, Nicki was well aware that some of her younger cousins considered her to be a straitlaced coldhearted you-know-what herself. They didn't understand.

Maybe she didn't understand Uncle James.

"True or not," she said, "I wasn't crazy about having it pointed out to everybody in the city that my father was a drug addict who raised his daughter as a street performer."

She flinched just saying it out loud. Giving voice to the words was her way of declaring that the truth had no power over her. Maybe someday, if she said it enough, it might be true.

"It's not like anybody was going to blame you because Uncle David was, you know, sick. And a lousy father."

Nicki glanced at Toni. Her young cousin was a Reynard, from the top of her mane of wild red hair to the tips of the toes she had shoved into a pair of size-ten snakeskin boots dyed red and purple. She also had the kind of husky throbbing singing voice that could give a saint a hard-on, a body the far side of Marilyn Monroe and an outspokenness saved from insensitivity only because she was always on target.

Nicki would have given the dimple in her chin to be more like Toni. But she knew full well that wasn't going to happen. She was what she was.

"You're a singer," she said to Toni. "Dysfunctional's trendy in the entertainment world right now. It doesn't play as well for family-court judges.''

''Not good for people to get the idea their family-court judges are human, huh?''

Nicki felt her anger rising all over again. What was she thinking, trying to have a conversation about the darkest demons of her life with an eighteen-year-old? ''Go to hell.''

Toni chuckled. She didn't have a temper, either. Some women had it all, Nicki thought. The rest of them got the leftovers. ''Yeah, probably. But not right away, if it's all the same to you.''

''I'll buy your ticket myself if you leave today and get off my back.''

Then they were both laughing. Nicki could almost forget that her Maman Riva, the closest thing she'd ever had to a responsible parent in her entire life, was consorting with Scott Lyon. The same Scott Lyon who had pointed a television camera at her face while one of his colleagues asked questions about the secrets she hid in the darkest corner of her soul. She could almost forget that he had found her hideaway, the place she'd gone to lick her wounds when the world found out that Judge Nicolette Bechet was not perfect.

She could almost forget that traitorous moment today when she'd felt a thrill at the sight of him.

"Come on," Toni said when their laughter subsided. "I've got to take Mom to her shrink today. If you come with me, I won't be tempted to draw mustaches on all the photographs on the covers of *Psychology Today* in the waiting room."

"I've got work to do," Nicki protested. "If I don't—"

Toni stood. "Looks like he's going to be here awhile."

Nicki glanced toward the house. The lemonade pitcher was out. His chair was edged close to Riva's, their foreheads almost touching as they talked. He did, indeed, look as if he was settling in.

"She's probably convinced him to wait you out."

Nicki didn't relish a battle of wills with her grandmother.

"My truck's at the cabin," Toni said. "We won't even have to go up to the house."

"Deal. I'll help you with the mustaches."

THEY WERE GONE all day. The look of shock on Aunt Cheryl's face when she saw Nicki's overalls and ball cap made the decision worthwhile. And at dusk, when Toni pulled into Cachette en Bayou's back driveway and parked near the cabin, Nicki took satisfaction in knowing she'd managed to outmaneuver the Lyon family once again.

Dinner had already begun on the back terrace. Nicki heard the talk and saw the flicker of candlelight when she tramped through the overgrown path from the cabin, along the swamp's edge, toward the house. Thank goodness that at Cachette en Bayou there was no need to dress for dinner. As she approached the shadowy terrace, she pulled off her ball cap and ran her fingers through her hair. She could smell the *étouffée* and her mouth began to water. Her cousin T-John must have rolled in this afternoon. T-John, who ran a modest little café in New Iberia, made the best *étouffée* in the county.

Nicki walked onto the terrace with a smile on her face. The cacophony of voices didn't change when she approached; she heard snatches of at least three conversations—one about the next season's rice crop, one about the latest crooked politician sweet-talking the voters, one about T-John's weight gain since his last visit. She made her way to her usual spot at the table.

Directly across from her empty chair sat Scott Lyon. He rose as she approached, a gentlemanly gesture never seen at the Bechet dinner table.

The candlelight flickered across his face, highlighting all the crisp angles. She couldn't tell that his eyes were gray in this light. But she remembered.

"You—"

"Hey, Nicki!" T-John's deep baritone cut through the rest of the noise at the table. "You near 'bout let these sorry cousins o' yours clean up the last of the *étouffée*. Beau, you pass that girl some food. And don't be taking more yourself. Nicki, Maman says you're going to help the big-shot Lyon family. How 'bout that? You gonna be on the news some?"

Nicki opened her mouth to deny it. But Riva's hand covered hers. Scott's eyes would not release her. And Perdu, from his place of honor on Riva's shoulder, said, "Shut up."

Good advice. She took it.

CHAPTER THREE

NICKI CLOSED the window of her third-story bed-
room to shut out the sounds of music and laughter coming from the cabin a few hundred yards
away.

The cabin hugging the water's edge saw some
partying almost every night, what with five cousins and a variety of long- and short-term signif-
icant others. Cold beer and hot music were routine at the place, but T-John's presence always
kicked things up a notch. T-John had stories to
tell and a big booming voice for telling them.
Tonight, the partying was louder and would go
on longer than usual, Nicki knew. She saw a
flicker through the trees, a signal someone had
started a bonfire. They would play their music
and sing in its light and its warmth.

Nicki turned away from the window. Riva
stood in the doorway, clutching the lapels of her
plum-colored silk robe with one gnarled hand, a
candleholder with the other. Perdu sat in his fa-

vorite spot and the dog flopped to the floor at her feet. In the flickering candlelight, her face was a dry riverbed of cracks and crevices.

"Nothing to be afraid of in having a little fun, *chère fille*." Her voice was soft this time of night. Nicki usually assumed it was weariness overcoming her grandmother, but sometimes she liked to pretend it was simply a special voice the old woman saved for her firstborn grandchild when they were alone.

"It isn't fun to me," Nicki replied, picking up the book she was reading.

"You are too serious for one so young."

"Not so young, Maman."

Riva made a dismissive sound and tapped her forehead. "Up here, not so young. Always up here, not so young."

It was true, but having it pointed out made Nicki uncomfortable. Having someone, even her grandmother, read her so easily made her uneasy. As did the high spirits of her cousins. She'd been around such frivolity all her life, growing up on the streets of New Orleans's French Quarter. Drunken laughter and boozy music were her heritage, courtesy of her father. But whenever she was around too much of it for too long, anxiety stirred in her, and then an urge to flee.

At times like that she felt ten again, and on guard against some unseen predator lurking beneath the music and the laughter.

She shrugged the feeling off. She understood her hang-ups. She could deal with them. "You should get your rest, Maman."

Riva smiled. "Me, I am lucky to sleep a few hours at my age. Too many young ones to worry about. And none of them settling down so I can rest easy."

Nicki thought about her cousins and returned her grandmother's smile. "They're a long way from settling down. Except Beau, I suppose."

"And you?"

"Me? I'm settled down."

Riva frowned.

"I am," Nicki insisted. "I have work I enjoy, helping others. I'm fixing up the house. You should be glad of that. The house will be here for all of us. It will keep us together."

"Bah! This old house. It will keep you a prisoner. It should fall down around us. That I would be glad of."

Nicki had never understood her grandmother's apparent aversion to the farm. "Why do you say that?"

"I go now. I must sleep, an old woman like me."

"You never answer my questions. Do you know that?"

Shuffling down the hall to her room, Riva cackled. The only reply came from Perdu, his usual "Shut up."

Nicki thought, not for the first time, that her grandmother seemed as restless and discontent sometimes as her father had always seemed. So much alike, yet they'd been constantly at odds. David Bechet had refused to be in the same room with his mother for most of Nicki's childhood. Nicki always thought that was her father's fault, or the fault of the drugs that had finally done him in.

Having lived with Riva these past two years, she had decided there might be more to it than that.

She plumped the pillows on her bed and lit the kerosene lamp she'd brought up for her bedside table. She stretched out her legs under the covers and opened the book, a techno-thriller that had proved to be a powerful sedative.

Tonight she listened to the pulsing beat of the music from the cabin. Tonight, she thought of the stories she was missing and the camaraderie she was rejecting.

Tonight, she thought of Scott Lyon. She thought of the way his pale eyes had searched her face across the dinner table, the way his smile flashed when T-John told one of his stories. His body looked lean and sculpted. And the tiny gold hoop in his ear signaled a certain rebelliousness that made Nicki wary. She remembered the way he closed his eyes and threw his head back, savoring the first bite of T-John's bread pudding. A man who liked his pleasures.

She thought of the way he'd rescued her two years ago and wondered why he'd done it.

Well, she would never know because she had no intention of having that kind of conversation with him.

She finished her book, but by the next morning couldn't remember how it had ended.

GOOD LORD, IT HAD BEEN a long time since he'd greeted the morning with a hangover. He wasn't one to overindulge, but it wasn't easy saying no to the Bechet family.

He pressed fingertips against his grainy eyes and sat up on the edge of the lumpy cot that had felt like heaven at about four in the morning.

Now it felt like a chiropractor's conspiracy to increase business. The chilled cabin was still littered with signs of recent habitation—messy cots, pillows and blankets piled up on chairs, a sleeping bag sprawled in the corner.

Apparently Scott and the person in the sleeping bag were the only ones who hadn't already risen. She blinked at him, revealing bright green eyes.

"Head hurt?"

He recognized the husky voice. Toni of the wet-dream body and the wild red hair. *If she's such a hot number,* he asked himself, *why were you thinking about Nicki all night?*

Because he didn't go after eighteen-year-old kids, his beer-befuddled brain replied.

Maybe that was it. Or maybe it wasn't.

"Head?" he muttered.

"That throbbing thing between your ears," she said, struggling out of the sleeping bag. She still wore her jeans from the night before. She didn't look any the worse for wear. That was the difference between eighteen and thirty-four, he reminded himself.

"Oh, that."

She stood and reached for his hand. "Come on. Maman Riva has a sure cure for hangovers.

Oyster juice, tomato juice, pepper sauce and raw egg.''

Scott took her hand and groaned. ''Not if I see it coming first.''

Toni laughed. ''Nobody ever sees Riva coming in time.''

Amazingly the massive cypress dining table on the brick terrace was already crowded when he and Toni arrived. Apparently the members of the Bechet clan were better trained than he was for the night's festivities. There didn't appear to be a queasy belly or a pounding head in the bunch.

''Ah, Scotty the Lion rises to greet the day!'' T-John's friendly greeting almost took the top off Scott's head. ''Maman, he is in need of elixir.''

Riva took Scott's hand and looked up into eyes he feared were bloodshot. ''Ah, you bad ones, what have you done to our visitor? Keep him up all night and pour liquor down his neck, I doubt not. Never mind, Riva will fix.''

''Please, Mrs. Bechet, that's not—'' she was already out of her chair and headed for the house ''—necessary.''

They all laughed. But the laughter was good-natured and it included him, drawing him once again into the circle of warmth that surrounded the Bechet cousins.

Except for one.

Nicki hadn't joined the partying the night before—Toni had explained that she seldom did—so Scott tried to believe her absence had nothing to do with him. And she wasn't here this morning. Riva answered his unspoken question when she returned, setting a glass before him.

"That one, she is already harassing the workmen. Drink up."

Scott glanced into the glass. His nose wrinkled involuntarily.

"If you have to eat a bullfrog," Riva said, "it is best not to stare at it too long."

Scott sipped.

Riva shook her head. "No sips. Gulp."

Beau added his encouragement. "The way you downed that first beer last night."

"Leave him be, you," Riva admonished. "This one, he's not a drunken lout like the bunch of you. Now, Scott, do like I say. Big swallow."

Riva was right. This bullfrog was gaining warts by the second. Scott held his breath, took a long gulp and downed three-fourths of the tomato-juice concoction. He didn't upchuck. He took that as a good sign.

The table broke out in applause when he set the empty glass back on the table.

"Now there's a real man," Tony declared. "Welcome to the bayou, city boy. You're all right."

Now that he'd downed the evil potion, Scott began both to relax and to feel better. He enjoyed three biscuits, scalding black coffee and the same kind of loving sharp-edged banter he had enjoyed the night before at the cabin. This, he thought, was family. Close. Warm. Loving. They enjoyed each other's company and there wasn't a phony in the bunch. Nothing formal or distant here, nothing reeking of the resentment that was always front-and-center at any Lyon family gathering.

Unless you counted Nicki, of course. He finished eating, insisted on helping Riva clear the table and wash up, then went in search of her.

She wasn't hard to find. He followed the sounds of a very vocal disagreement, and sure enough, there she was, knee-deep in workmen and leading with her chin.

"I'll not have any second-rate carpentry on this house, Em. It gets done right or it gets done by someone else."

The workman who had spoken to Scott when he'd first arrived the day before stood almost nose to nose with Nicki, massive paws on his hips. He should have dwarfed her, but somehow didn't. She stood tall and straight in a pair of white canvas painter's pants and a blue-and-white striped T-shirt.

"I never do nothing second-rate. Emile Lafitte is the best, and I tell you, two-by-fours will do the job. Any man will know this."

"Don't patronize me, you big ugly Cajun. It's my house and I want four-by-fours." Her voice remained calm and firm, despite the growing rage in Emile's voice.

The man rolled his eyes. "This is waste. This is damn fool woman talk."

"Four-by-fours," Nicki repeated, still calm, still firm.

"Twice the money," Em countered.

"I can get it done for half."

Em gasped as if he'd been slapped. "Do that and you see what second-rate really looks like, you. No, third rate!"

"I'll take my chances."

Nicki turned and walked away.

Em groaned, raised his hands toward heaven, muttered a prayer that might actually have been a curse if Scott had been able to understand his Cajun French. "Four-by-fours, you mule-headed woman. You get four-by-fours. I lose money, but you get your way. Now, happy?''

Nicki didn't slow down. ''I'll let you know when I see the work done.''

Em muttered some more; the knot of workmen began to drift back to their jobs. Em spotted Scott, shook his head and jabbed a finger in the direction of Scott's chest. ''I tell you this, that woman…that woman…a gentleman can't say about that woman. You ever see a woman like that?''

She was pausing along the way now, encouraging the other workers, passing out kudos and smiles. She seemed completely unaffected by the argument with Emile, showed no sign she was gloating over her victory.

''Can't say that I have,'' Scott replied. But as soon as he'd said it, he realized it wasn't true.

Nicolette Bechet was a younger, earthier version of Aunt Margaret. *One tough broad.* That was what Aunt Margaret sometimes called herself. He thought she might say the same of Nicki if she ever met her. If he ever saw his aunt again.

A wave of melancholy swept over him. Big *if*s.

But the tough woman disappearing into the house might be the key to turning those *if*s into

*when*s. Shoving away the melancholy and grabbing onto the slim hope that rested with Nicki
Bechet, he followed her into the house. She was
in conversation with one of the electricians, and
this confrontation was quite subdued. Scott suspected that only an old friend like Emile Lafitte
would dare to do battle with Nicki. Watching the
electrician agree to whatever Nicki was request-
ing, Scott had no doubt that the Bechet clan
would continue to be a matriarchy, long after
Riva Reynard Bechet went on to her reward.

Nicki seemed to notice Scott for the first time
after the electrician went back to his work. For a
moment her confident air appeared to evaporate.
But the fleeting vulnerability vanished so quickly
Scott wondered if he'd imagined it. Imagined that
she reacted to him as strongly, and as inexpli-
cably, as he reacted to her.

"I suppose you want me to help you now,"
she said.

He'd watched a lot of men back down in the
face of Aunt Margaret's toughness. One who
hadn't, he recalled, was her husband, Uncle Paul.
"That's right."

"Might as well get this over with."

She led him to a room farther down the hall.
It was small, and made even smaller by the

mountains of stuff—an old wooden door set atop sawhorses for a makeshift desk, an old-fashioned wooden swivel chair, a wall of gray metal shelves stacked with books and files and newspapers, with more of the same spilled onto the floor beneath the only window. Two marble-based brass floor lamps curved like vultures over the desk. A padlocked steamer trunk was shoved behind the door and almost obscured by more books and papers. A blown-glass wind chime tinkled beside the open window. The only thing in the room that fit his image of Nicolette Bechet was the state-of-the-art computer, printer and fax machine on the door/desk.

She sat in the chair, picked up one of about five hundred spiral-bound notebooks in the room, unerringly located a ballpoint pen in the chaos and looked at him.

"Sorry. Only one chair in my office and it's mine." She was crisp and automatic. The impassioned woman who didn't mind wrangling with a carpenter had vanished. Scott found the transformation intriguing.

He dropped to the floor and sat at her feet. "No problem. I always think it's wise for a man to look up to a woman."

He smiled. She frowned.

"The power's off for the electrical work and I can't fire up Sam. So—"

"Sam?"

Her frown deepened. She tipped her head in the direction of the computer. "So what I suggest is—"

"I never knew a computer with a name before."

She tapped the ballpoint against the notebook. She gave him a look like those the nuns had given him in school when he'd disrupted the class.

"Well, now you do. Here's what—"

"Sam what?"

She was biting the inside of her lip. To keep from losing her temper, he supposed.

"Spade."

"I get it. Sam Spade, private detective. The two of you find people."

"You're quick, Mr. Lyon. I'm impressed. Now can we get on with this?"

"Oh, sure." He smiled again. He supposed, actually, he'd been smiling all along. His hangover must be gone. "She should patent it."

"What?"

"Maman Riva's Hangover Potion."

Judging by the grip she had on the pen, it

should snap any moment. That wasn't going to help her mood at all. He reached up and touched her fingers. "You're tense, Nicki. Do I make you nervous?"

She flinched away. "Yes. People who prey on others make me nervous."

"And I prey on others?"

"You're a Lyon, aren't you?"

He met the challenge in her eyes, but refused to match her bristling attitude. He'd been catching it one way or another all his life for being a Lyon. He was too rich for those who had less. He was too stingy for those who wanted a handout. He was too privileged, too powerful, too driven. He was none of those things, of course. He'd made a point not to be, in fact. And he'd also made a point of never defending himself against assumptions.

"I was glad you got away that night," he said, instead.

That stopped her for a moment. He saw the speculation behind those ice-blue eyes, but he knew before she spoke that she wouldn't give voice to her curiosity. "I can't imagine why it mattered to you."

The edge in her voice was intended to veil the

unspoken question. Scott believed he'd keep the judge guessing.

"Margaret Lyon doesn't prey on people," he said, turning the conversation back to the reason he was here.

The other reason.

"I'm sure."

"Trust me."

"Absolutely. Now about your aunt—I'll need some details so that when Sam is back in commission I can do a little nosing around."

He gave her what details he could and promised to get back to her with the information he didn't have. Margaret's social security number and her parents' dates of birth. He supposed he could get it all from his cousin Gaby or her daughter Leslie. He wasn't sure how any of it would help Nicki find a woman no one else could find. But he was here and he wanted to come back, so he would simply do what she asked.

She slapped the notebook shut and tossed it onto the desktop together with the pen. She was poised to stand. He was being dismissed, free to return to the city, to WDIX-TV, to his squabbling family.

"Why do you do this?"

"How is that relevant?" she countered.

He reminded himself of what he knew of her, of the scandal that had first placed her in his path. A father dead of a drug overdose, a less-than-stable childhood. Street performers, if he remembered correctly. That was what made her so brittle. Her past and his role in exposing it.

"Interesting, not relevant."

"If it isn't relevant, I don't have time for it. You may have noticed I have a lot of work to do."

She stood and stepped over him, then waited at the door for him. He decided not to be any more trying to her than he'd already been. "I'll bring the rest of the information tomorrow."

He paused at the door. The expression in her eyes should have cooled everything in the vicinity—including him—but somehow it didn't. The aloofness was at odds with the unruly dance of her curls, which made his fingers ache with need. He wanted to bury his hands in her hair. To lose himself in the heat he felt despite the chill she projected.

"Call, Mr. Lyon. A phone call will be fine."

A call would be preferable was what she meant, he knew.

"I don't mind the drive," he said.

"Don't push me, Lyon. You aren't welcome

on my land or in my life. I don't know how to be any clearer than that."

Scott wasn't one to push. But pushing back, that was different. A man had an obligation to push back, didn't he?

"Can I kiss you goodbye?"

Color rushed into her cheeks, anger more than embarrassment, he speculated. She clenched a fist and he thought for a moment he was going to find out what kind of right hook she had.

"On second thought, maybe I won't help you at all."

Obviously getting past this woman's defenses was going to take some doing, and he knew he wasn't advancing his cause one bit.

"Is that a no to the kiss, too?" he asked, matching her determination with a cocksureness of his own.

"My shotgun's still loaded."

"I guess that's a definite no."

"This isn't a game, Lyon."

"No. It isn't."

He saw the shudder of anxiety tighten her face when she realized what he meant. It wasn't a game, a flirtation, a seduction. She knew now what he'd known for two years. He wanted her. And she didn't appear pleased at the news.

CHAPTER FOUR

RAYMOND LYON suppressed a belch.

The food at Chez Charles always gave him heartburn, but he didn't complain about it much. Maybe there was no such thing as a free lunch for the rest of the world, but the rules were a little different when your father owned the joint.

"We oughtta fix this place up, hire somebody who can actually cook, when the old man croaks," Ray said.

He watched his older brother wipe his fingers on a white linen napkin and screw up his face as if he smelled something bad. Alain was like the old man in that way, always acting as if he was above the rest of them. Ray supposed it ran in the family; most of the Lyons seemed to behave that way.

"Have a modicum of class, why don't you, Raymond."

Alain's hoity-toity attitude ticked Ray off. He

decided to bring up the one topic that would upset his brother. "I moved the old lady again."

Alain glanced around. He had a full head of
hair, touched with silver at the temples, the perfect hint of dignity for a man pushing fifty,
whereas Raymond, who wasn't even forty yet,
already had a hole in his haircut, right at the
crown of his head. Life wasn't fair.

"Not here," Alain said.

Ray ignored him. "To Arkansas. Close enough
to keep an eye on her."

"How is she?"

Ray shrugged. "Old. How good can she be?
You know, she could kick any time. And that
might not be a bad—"

"She'd better not," Alain said with the au-
thoritarian tone that always made Ray want to do
just the opposite.

"Might simplify things."

"And it might blow up in somebody's face."

Ray knew what that meant. Somebody's face,
as in not Alain's. Alain was in this up to his
prissy red suspenders, but Ray knew that the
smoking gun would lead right back to him, and
only him, if their little scheme was ever uncovered. Damn. Alain was wily. Slick. And Ray was

just the stupid kid brother, the way it had always been.

"You're the one who said it wasn't a good idea to keep her in one place too long," Ray reminded him.

"I didn't say you had to put her in a dump."

"You have any idea how many questions they ask at first-class nursing homes? They practically want your fingerprints and a sign-off from the pope."

"All right. All right. Just make sure nothing happens to her."

The waiter refilled their coffee. Alain made small talk with him, all smiles, a prince of a fellow.

"Well, if that's all..." Alain folded his napkin and placed it beside his plate when the waiter moved on to the next table. Ray was being dismissed, and not even as politely as the pretty-boy waiter.

"Scott took off." Ray liked bringing a troubled look to his brother's face.

"What do you mean?"

"I mean he left the station right after the assignment meeting yesterday and he wasn't back this morning. Nobody's heard from him."

Ray knew his news would bother Alain. Scott

wasn't exactly on the team regarding this legal action they'd taken against André. Of course, Alain also thought they were going to need Scott when it came time to run the station because Scott was the only one of the four of them who knew beans about broadcasting. As if Ray—who had been at the station forever—was chopped liver. He could see it now. When the station finally belonged to them, Alain would probably make Scotty news director. Or worse, general manager.

Ray winced with his heartburn.

"Did you check his apartment?"

"What am I, his keeper?"

Alain's face grew sour again.

"Word is he may quit," Ray said.

"I'll talk to him. Apply a little pressure."

That sounded good to Ray. Because if he knew one thing about his little brother Scotty, the kid didn't fold under pressure. In fact, if Alain pushed, Scotty would most likely become more stubborn than ever. If Alain said stick by the family, Scotty would turn his back on all of them. And that was fine with Ray. He wouldn't mind it one bit if Scotty took himself out of the running just when things were going their way. That would leave a bigger slice of the pie for him.

NICKI PAINTED so furiously her right arm was giving out and she hadn't come close to covering the four third-story dormers on the second wing of the house. The pitch of the roof was steep, and two coats of sage-green were necessary to cover the ugly mud-gray paint that some taste-challenged ancestor had chosen.

And everyone at Cachette en Bayou apparently felt—and indulged—the urge to interrupt her.

"Nick-o!" That was T-John, hanging out a dormer window.

"You're smudging my paint," she replied.

He looked down at his T-shirt. "No harm done. Listen, Nick-o, you sent the city boy packing?"

She turned back to her painting. "I certainly did."

"We like him."

"I don't."

"Well, hell, girl. You lock yourself in the tower every night anyway."

She denied it automatically. T-John snorted disrespectfully.

"I think you do like him. And that's why you shipped his cute little buns back to N'Awlins."

"You think he's got cute little buns? He's yours, T-John. Just keep him off my farm."

"Okay, okay. I just came to file a protest. And give you a reality check."

"Consider my reality checked."

Thank goodness, she thought as T-John backed away and left her in peace, she wasn't one to get worked up over a man with a nice backside or any other physical attributes. Granted, she'd noticed Scott's gray eyes and his elegantly molded face. But she wasn't into lust. Thank goodness.

Michel came next. "Word to the woman," he said. "You're getting pushy. We all live here, you know. You don't have the sole right to open or close the castle gate. Do I make myself clear?"

What was clear was Michel's resentment of Nicki's leadership role in the family. As the oldest male grandchild, he thought he should be in charge, and Nicki and everyone else should defer to him. Which might be fine if he didn't think every other day should be declared a beer-drinking holiday.

"Pick up a paintbrush, Mikie. I'm willing to share."

"You've got a sharp tongue, Nicki. You know that don't you?"

"I think you told me that for the first time in 1984."

"Yeah, well, nothing's changed."

Beau came next, sticking his head out the window and sharing much the same opinion as his brothers. Tony didn't show because he hated heights. But after Beau retreated Toni came up, crawled onto the roof with Nicki and slapped around a paintbrush for an hour or so, although she left as much sage-green on the roof as she left on the outside walls.

"He's nice," Toni said after a companionable silence. "I thought he might not be, being rich and all. But he's regular. Kind of quiet, but nice."

Nicki considered the possibility Scott had been spying on her and her family and was plotting to use whatever information he gleaned. But she knew that sounded—and probably was—incredibly paranoid, so she kept it to herself.

"He's too old for you," she replied, instead.

"Oh, I know that. He's got *gray* hair, for goodness' sake! I just meant, I don't think he's got, like, any ulterior motives."

"You might be naive, even for an eighteen-year-old," Nicki said tartly.

"I think he's just lonely and I think he needs your help, Nick-chick."

Their painting resumed in uneasy silence.

Nicki fumed. Why was everyone in her family so all-fired determined to take Scott Lyon into the fold? She might have known he'd charm them all. What was he up to? What was behind those magnetic eyes of his?

She heard the spare brush Toni was using hit the drop cloth. She looked up in time to see her young cousin brushing her hands on the thighs of her jeans. "Gotta run. We're rehearsing at three. A gig over in Ponchatoula Saturday night."

"Yeah? You guys are doing all right, aren't you?"

Toni shrugged, but she looked pleased. "It's giving Mom and Dad a cow, though. You know, their baby girl playing in little swamp houses. Dad offered me a year in Europe if I'd give it up."

"No dice, huh?"

"No dice." Toni swung a long leg through the window and straddled it for a moment. "I mean, I'll be glad to settle down one day. Have babies. When I'm too old for jiving around."

"Settling down or jiving around aren't the only options in the world, Toni."

"Yeah. I suppose I could be like you."

Nicki stared at her young cousin. "What's wrong with being like me?"

"Sometimes you're a drone, okay? You never have fun. You also don't seem to have any, I don't know, passion for anything. You know?"

Yes. Nicki knew. It stung that an eighteen-year-old could see it so plainly. Her fist tightened around her paintbrush. "Somebody's got to..." She floundered.

"Got to what, Nicki?"

Everything she could think to say reinforced Toni's judgment. "Somebody's got to paint the damn house!"

"We could all help," Toni said. "We could have a painting party. T-John could organize a crawfish boil and we could have a little music, and in no time—"

"Not everything's a party, Toni."

Nicki jabbed her brush into the bucket and slapped at the wall, splattering herself and the roof and the nearby shutter.

"You're right, Nick-stick. Everything isn't a party. But some things are. And if I can't exactly be perfectly balanced, well, I guess I know which direction I'd rather lean toward."

"We aren't all alike."

Nicki tried to keep her voice steady, tried not

..veal the sorrow welling up in her as she saw her life reflected in Toni's words. Toni put a hand on Nicki's wrist and she glanced at her cousin. Toni was smiling at her; her eyes held sympathy. Nicki didn't want to see that.

"But we love each other, anyway," Toni said softly.

Nicki felt some of her defenses crumble. "Yes," she replied. "We love each other, anyway."

"Well, listen, I'm outta here. Kiss-kiss."

Nicki blew a kiss at Toni as she slipped back into the house.

Feeling deflated by the conversation with her cousin, Nicki sat beside the bucket and rubbed at the paint splatters on her cheeks and nose. From this perch, she had a wide-ranging view of Bechet land. A wooded thicket clung to the edges of the clearing, snuggling up to the house. Spanish moss hung like a veil, shielding the house and its occupants from whatever the outside world held. The silence of the dense swampland wrapped itself around Nicki, comforting her as it always had.

As a child, she had loved sitting on the roof when she'd managed to run away from her father and make her way to Cachette en Bayou.

Hideaway on the bayou. The words had played in her mind like magic during her childhood. When she was here, she felt safe. And when she wasn't here, it beckoned to her.

She'd grown up in the French Quarter, abandoned by her teenage mother at the age of four, left in the care of her party-time father. David Bechet had been a rebel, a hippie and a pothead when it was cool to be those things. He was also a musician and a young man driven by the compulsion to hurt his mother.

David stayed in the Quarter with his daughter, raised her as neglectfully as one might expect from a pothead musician. He saw that she was fed, most of the time, but her presence never got in the way of his drugs or his music or his own personal sexual revolution. School became Nicki's favorite retreat, but the summers were long and miserable, especially when her father took to earning his bread as a street musician for the tourists who flocked to the Quarter. He played a mournful saxophone and a wicked fiddle. He taught his daughter to dance and pass the hat.

"You always up the take, half-pint," he would tell her, jocularly at first, more belligerently when she began refusing to participate. She hated the noise and the jostling crowds and the smells of booze and drugs and the way people looked at her. Pity from the motherly women and something worse from a few of the men.

So she ran away. Repeatedly. Usually to her grandmother, who always sent her home to her father no matter how much she begged and pleaded.

"A child belongs with her parent," Maman Riva said, her pointed chin jutting forward.

Nicki quit begging and pleading after a while. But she never quit running away.

Until now. She didn't have to run anymore because she had made it back to the safe place. And that was all she'd ever wanted out of life.

Scott Lyon and his television station weren't going to rob her of that.

SCOTT SHOULD HAVE EXPECTED to hear from Alain when he decided to opt out of the family dinner with Papa and his brothers. Family loyalty was the Lyon brothers' code, as long as you were careful which side of the family tree you hung your loyalty on.

Beneath the golden glow of the streetlights, Alain's long sleek car stood out among the shabbier vehicles in the parking lot in front of Scott's town house. It wasn't parked in a marked space, for one thing. It was idling in the middle of the lot. Rules were for other people. Another Lyon family belief.

Scott parked in his spot. He'd spent the evening alone, brooding over a silent movie being screened at one of the media superstores in town. Cappuccino bar, books and headphones for listening to every CD in the joint. Nothing was simple anymore, not even bookstores. But he'd enjoyed the quiet in the viewing room and had brought his peaceful mind-set home with him.

He wasn't going to let Alain spoil it.

He walked over to his brother's car. The tinted window lowered silently. "Slumming, Alain?" he asked.

Alain smiled benignly. "Making sure my baby brother's okay. We're concerned."

"I'm fine."

"You've missed some work. Didn't make dinner tonight. That isn't like you, Scott."

Scott saw no point in dancing around it. "I'm tired of work. No, I'm tired of the bickering. I don't want to hear it at work and I sure don't want to hear it sitting around the dinner table at that gloomy old museum we grew up in."

"You sound bitter."

"Maybe I am."

"It's a difficult time for all of us."

"Funny. You and Ray look pretty pleased with yourselves over all this crap."

"We need to stick together. The family needs you."

Scott knew there was no point whatsoever in mentioning that André was also family.

"And when all this is settled," Alain said, "the station is going to need you, too."

Ah. At last his brother's concern made sense. They'd need his expertise until they could figure out how to run a television station. He hated the way his brothers always put a price tag on relationships. Your value to the family was measured by how much you could do for them.

He shook his head. "I don't think so. I'm through with the family business."

"Now, Scott, don't be foolish. What else can you do? You'll be a valuable part of the team once the legal wrangling is over. Don't forget that."

"I don't want to be part of your team. I don't want to be part of the legal wrangling. I'd like to be part of a family, but that doesn't seem to be an option."

"Aren't you being a little melodramatic?"

If Alain wanted melodrama, Scott was ready for him. "I'm quitting the station."

"You'll change your mind."

"You'll manage without me." He turned to go. He was too close to losing the peace of mind he'd worked for this evening.

"You can't resign from family," Alain called out.

"Watch me."

He unlocked the door of his town house and closed it behind him without sparing another look for the brother he had once worshiped.

The soft light from a corner reading lamp was the only illumination in the room. He left it that way. The main floor of his town house was basically one room, an L-shaped living area and breakfast nook separated from a compact kitchen by an off-white tile-topped bar. Black appliances, two black leather recliners, a smoke-colored glass-topped dining table and a bronze baker's rack for his stereo equipment and another for books, all against a palette of warm gold-on-gold wallpaper, reflected his uncluttered life. He tossed his ball cap into one of the recliners, fired up one of his favorite CDs and went to the kitchen to make a pot of decaf.

The soft classical music soothed him all over

again. It reminded him of his childhood, the early years before family resentments were apparent to him, before he'd become aware that his parents' marriage was a sham. His father always played classical music on the piano, turning the keyboard into something magical. For a while so had Alain.

Alain was fifteen years older than Scott, and that automatically elevated him in a little boy's eyes to something akin to a god. Alain was on the debating team, he was in the best fraternity at his university, and he squired around the prettiest women.

And Alain taught his baby brother things. He taught him that their cousin André was a backstabber. He taught him how poor they were compared to André's side of the family. He taught him a detailed family history about their father's shabby treatment at the hands of his own father, resulting in the loss of their rightful inheritance.

Alain taught Scott all those things. But by the time he was ten or twelve, some of those things no longer seemed right.

André wasn't a backstabber. In fact, he had more time and encouragement for young Scott than anyone else in the family except Aunt Margaret. Scott's side of the family was far from poor, although his father did manage to squander whatever profits Chez Charles earned; André and his father, Paul, were always there with another handout. That was the real truth. And far from having been chased off, Charles had actually walked away from the family business after almost running the radio station into the ground.

Those were the facts, gleaned over the years from his mother and others in the family.

But Alain, Raymond and, to some extent, Jason had never let the facts get in the way of their jealousy and their determination to one day have what they believed was rightfully theirs.

Scott loved his brothers. And he hated what they'd done to his family.

The coffeepot quit gurgling. He filled his favorite mug, doctored it with the barest hint of milk and a generous sprinkling of cinnamon and sugar. He let the warmth seep into his chest just as the music was filling his head and his heart with quiet.

Maybe he would read. Maybe he would douse the lights, sip his decaf and let Pachelbel lull him to sleep.

The doorbell rang before he could sit.

Alain again? Who else would be at his door at

this hour? Scott was a loner. He sometimes forgot he had a doorbell.

Reluctantly he opened the door. Riva Bechet
looked taller and straighter than he'd remembered her.

"You look different without Perdu on your
shoulder," he said.

She chuckled. "Most people think I look different *with* Perdu on my shoulder."

She looked different, period, he thought as he
ushered her in. She wore a red-and-purple serape,
dashingly draped over a black leotard and a full
skirt in a bold print of green, yellow and purple.
Her hair was tied up in a black-and-gold scarf.
Her earrings were turquoise and lapis. She sank
into one of the recliners, accepted a mug of coffee and closed her eyes as if she had made her
last move for the night.

"How very nice," she said, opening her eyes
again. "Masculine. But comfortable."

"Thank you."

"You doubt I am coming all this way for small
talk."

"It does seem unlikely."

She smiled. "Still, it might be I would come
all this way for one of these chairs. Bless my

soul, it's better than a rocker. Why they don't be telling us old folks that?''

She sipped her coffee. He studied her face, worn and weary. He was surprisingly hungry for contact with her and her family. And not just Nicki.

"You will have to push her, sure."

Scott wasn't accustomed to people being so straightforward. He found he liked it. "Why should I do that?"

"Because you need her."

"The Lyon family has a detective. The police, the FBI. I don't really—"

"Oh, yes, you do." She was hard to argue with. Her eyes seemed to see beyond him to things he couldn't yet grasp. "She needs you. But you will have to push her."

"Maybe you could take the shotgun away from her before I try that."

Riva laughed. "Maybe you could bargain with her."

"Bargain? How?"

"She puts down her gun—and helps with Mrs. Lyon. You help with her TV show."

"Her what?"

"A dream she has. Nicki, she wants to produce a documentary about people looking for parents who abandoned them.'' The old woman's face grew somber. In silence, she stared into her coffee.

Again Scott had a strong sense that she was looking deeply into places where he had not yet been granted passage. He waited out her silence.

At last Riva looked up. ''This is what drives her—a need to help these people so they can heal.''

The brief silence that followed that statement was also full of unspoken portent. This time, however, Scott could almost hear what was unsaid. So *Nicki* can heal.

He wanted to know more, but he wouldn't ask. Riva had already said more than Nicki would want him to know. The rest would have to come from Nicki herself, and only if he could earn her trust. He knew that was going to be difficult. He thought of Nicki's father, his unsavory death. Was there more? And did he have any right to dredge it up, even for Nicki's sake?

''It's that important to her?'' he asked. ''That she'd make a deal with the devil?''

''You are the devil?''

''She thinks I am.''

Riva finished her coffee, set the mug on the table and began to gather her serape around her.

"This you must work out yourself. You are a clever young man. Now you must excuse me. I am out too late. And if my grandchildren find me out, they will know I am not so frail and expect me to cook for them every night. That will never do."

He walked her to the cab sitting at the curb, offered to take her home himself, but discovered that the ancient cabbie was off duty, an old friend who treated Riva Bechet as if she were a queen. She was in good hands.

The last thing she said before he closed the door of the cab was, "I will see you tomorrow."

FIGHTING. SHE WAS SUPPOSED to be fighting, but she couldn't think why or what.

It was dark. Cold. Uncomfortable. She felt weak and unsure of herself, and she wasn't accustomed to feeling that way.

"My name..." she muttered into the darkness.

"What's that, dearie?"

The woman with the needle. Sweet voice, gentle touch. Except for the needle, which pricked, then brought oblivion. She tried to writhe away. She didn't need oblivion. She needed...answers.

She was too weak to elude the needle. Then

the sweet voice and the gentle touch left the room. She was alone again.

"Margaret," she said, grasping hold of what she'd wanted to say earlier. The only problem was, she'd already forgotten what it meant or why she felt the need to say it so urgently.

Never mind. She felt *him*. Felt his presence. Paul. A comfort. Strength.

Take me with you, she thought, her voice already too weak for more words.

But it wasn't time yet. He would stay with her until it was.

She wanted to cry. She didn't understand. She was so tired of struggling. She wanted to give up.

CHAPTER FIVE

NICKI'S MOMENTARY ELATION from the phone call ended as it always did—in deflation, hovering around the edges of discouragement.

Susan McKee's call was welcome of course. Her joyful recounting of her reunion with the mother who had given her up for adoption thirty-seven years earlier validated Nicki's work, the countless hours she spent on cold or nearly non-existent trails. When those trails led, as this one had, to an opportunity for a relationship between two people related by blood, Nicki knew the long hours in front of her computer screen were worth it. And even when the reunions didn't go well, she usually heard satisfaction in the voices of the people she helped, people who now had some answers to the questions they'd been asking for so long.

But when the last phone call was done, Nicki was once again left with nothing but a name and an empty aching heart.

Debra Brackett. DOB 9-18-48. Second daughter of Delmar and Alma Brackett of Lawndale, Mississippi. Married to Eddie Miller or Millner in 1970. Last known address, Oneonta, Alabama, 1973.

Nicki stared at her computer screen and resisted the urge to look at the photograph taped to the bottom of her computer keyboard. The Polaroid print had faded, the color no longer true, if indeed it ever had been. And she knew it by heart.

A very young Debra Brackett—she would have been eighteen, according to Nicki's father—held a toddler in her lap. They were on a bench at Audubon Park. The toddler looked fussy. The teenager's face was solemn, pinched. Her streaked blond hair hung long and straight below her shoulders. Her nose was slim, maybe a little too long for prettiness. She had a faraway look in her eyes.

Two years later she had left the child and taken off to wherever that faraway place was.

Nicki bit her lower lip and, for distraction, looked at the next form on her stack. Margaret Hollander Lyon. She shuffled it to the bottom.

Every time she found someone, she had to work her way out of an emotional slump that came with knowing her own mother continued to elude her. Where was Debra Brackett Miller? Barely past fifty, she should still be alive. She might have other children, half brothers and sisters to her first daughter. She might spend her nights as Nicki sometimes did, nursing a longing.

"If that's the case," Nicki muttered, "she could come after me."

After all, the Bechets weren't hard to find.

Debra Brackett obviously didn't want to see her daughter. Or she had another family now and didn't want anyone to know about her flower-child days in New Orleans. Nicolette Bechet was a dirty little secret.

Nicki stood up abruptly. She hated these moods, hated her self-pity, hated the woman who had rejected her and left her to be raised by a worthless excuse for a father. She stormed out of the tiny office that felt, for the moment, like a cage.

She made her way to the pier, distancing herself from the noise of construction and remodeling, the laughter and conversation between Aunt Simone and Maman Riva. She needed the soothing company of nature.

Two egrets entertained her for a while with their serene stillness. Then a mink appeared to warm itself in a patch of sunlight. Nicki closed her eyes and listened for the muted sounds of the swamp, a subtle music that sang to her in a way that jazz and zydeco never could.

She heard a footfall behind her, the heel of a shoe popping a twig, crushing a leaf. Her serenity fled.

The footsteps, when they reached the pier where she sat, were heavy. They belonged to a man. And despite the small army of men—cousins and carpenters, electricians and plumbers—currently roaming Cachette en Bayou, she knew exactly who this man was.

"I brought the rest of the information you wanted," he said. "About Aunt Margaret."

His voice had the same soothing quality as nature's soft whisper. But it couldn't override the other ways he unsettled her.

"I thought you understood," she said without turning. "I changed my mind."

"I came to change it back."

He approached and dropped down beside her on the pier, sat facing her with one long leg bent to provide a prop for his elbow. His ball cap dangled from his fingertips. His fingers were long, she noted, the nails carefully trimmed and scrupulously clean.

Never trust a man with clean hands, T-John always said. Of course, T-John's hands were immaculate. *How you think I know this?* he would add with a wicked grin.

"You can't change my mind," she said, determined not to let him rile her.

"How about we make a deal? I help you, you help me."

"I don't need your help."

"That's not what I hear."

"Then you have bad information."

She wished he wouldn't look at her so intently. She shifted slightly, suddenly feeling warm to her core. Yet he wasn't assessing her the way some men did, their eyes lingering on her lips or her breasts. No, Scott Lyon gazed into her eyes as if he might somehow see past them into her soul.

Nobody got that far with Nicki Bechet.

"I have a video camera," he said. "Access to editing equipment, sound mixing, contacts with people who could help syndicate a documentary."

Fury welled up in her chest. She swore vehemently and leapt to her feet.

"Grandmother!"

He looked up at her, apparently unperturbed

by her outburst. "I help you with your documentary, you help me find my aunt."

Even in the midst of feeling betrayed, she was tempted. She could almost see her documentary on the air now, touching hearts and providing hope for children separated from their parents. Snatches of narrative floated through her head, the expressions on the faces of the people she would interview. In her head, the project was alive.

In reality, she didn't have the experience or the wherewithal to get it done.

But help from Scott Lyon was out of the question.

"No."

Now walk away, she told herself. *Right now.*

But she didn't. She waited. Waited for his response. Waited to see what he would do next to convince her.

He stood in one fluid movement. He was tall, over six feet, but not as massively built as her cousins. Her heart began to pound a little harder.

"What's this about?" he asked, his voice still soft. If he'd been one of her cousins, they could have a nice knock-down-drag-out argument, go stomping off and be out of each other's hair.

But no, Scott Lyon was different. Scott Lyon behaved in ways she didn't know how to handle.

"I don't like your family!" she said, raising her voice to compensate for his calm. "Your family trampled all over my family, and you've got some nerve coming here expecting my help! That's what this is all about."

"That's not it." So softly she wanted to shove him in the swamp.

"What do you mean, that's not it! You arrogant SOB, I said that's it, so that's it!"

Leave! But she still couldn't obey the frantic inner voice. She could only stand and wait.

He moved closer. So close he seemed to suck up all the air that should have been hers, leaving her short of breath.

"There's something else," he said. "Why don't you tell me what it is?"

She could feel him, his heat and his strength, vibrating. Not only pervading the air around her, but seeping under her skin, filling her, overtaking her. In a moment he would be touching her. She knew it as surely as she knew his name.

And just as surely, she knew she would let him, would allow him to envelop her.

And then he would win.

She backed away, her anger dissipating into something more like fear.

Damn him all to hell and back.

She didn't move quickly enough. He edged up on her again. His hand was at the back of her head before she could react. He lowered his lips to hers. Her heart was bursting in her chest, and her thoughts had frozen. She lacked the will to pull away.

His lips were soft, as soft and warm as the mink lying in the patch of sunshine. They coaxed hers into moving against his, into admitting that she wanted his kiss. Her head was spinning, her body began to melt into his, and there seemed no way to stop it. She parted her lips, felt the faintest tease of his tongue along her lips. She gave in to the pull of his body, allowed herself to be pressed to his chest and abdomen. His free arm encircled her waist, held her securely.

For a split second she felt sure of her place in the world for the first time in her life. Her heart overflowed with emotions—and she knew she had to reject them.

She wrenched free of his grasp.

He made no attempt to hold on to her.

She stared at him, waiting for the smug expression she was certain would come into his eyes. It didn't.

"That's not going to change my mind, either," she said, panting, waiting for him to deliver some smooth line.

"No, I don't expect it will," he said. "But I was attracted to you two years ago and I still am. I think that's what has you running scared."

"You have no idea what you're talking about," she said, then turned and made her way back to the house as quickly as possible.

He was, however, right. His being attracted to her did frighten her. But knowing she wanted him, too, that was absolutely terrifying.

HE HADN'T LEFT.

The cousins staged a shrimp boil at the fishing cabin, scrubbing out the big black pot and hanging it over an open fire. Messes of shrimp and crawfish, fistfuls of firecracker-hot spices, chunks of onion and garlic were thrown into the pot. Then it was all eaten with bare fingers and crusty French bread, washed down with bottles of beer scooped out of a leaky washtub heaped with ice. With spontaneous music and laughter on the side.

Nicki didn't attend. She heated a can of soup

on the stove, poured it into a bowl and stared at it until it grew cold.

His kiss had broken her heart.

She'd had lovers before. But there had always been ground rules, established by her and sometimes known only by her. Career first, intimacy limited to that of a physical nature only. She didn't even ask herself why it needed to be that way. She knew.

Because everyone she'd ever needed to love her had rejected her.

Her mother, who ran away and took great pains never to be found again. Her father, who hid in his drugs and his partying. Maman Riva, who sent her back time and time again to her father.

And, of course, Steve Walthan. One of her second-year law professors. Well respected, financially stable, emotionally stable enough to appeal to a young woman who desperately needed someone strong and solid in her life. Unfortunately he'd been out of her league. He'd had no interest in a permanent relationship with a Cajun woman.

He'd been too smooth and too careful to say so straight out, of course. But even someone as naive and insecure as she had been at twenty-two could finally see the truth.

And she knew the truth about Scott Lyon, too. No way a member of the Lyon family was looking for anything more than a fling with someone like her.

Just then Riva came through the door off the terrace. "I thought we had the electricity back," she said, looking around the dark room and reaching for a switch.

Light flooded the room.

"Ah," Riva said. "You be brooding in the dark on purpose."

"You couldn't leave well enough alone, could you?"

Riva unwrapped her serape and let it fall into the arm of a chair. She went to the sideboard and poured a tiny glass of curaçao. "Me, I'm having a nightcap. You?"

"Why are you so anxious for me to find Margaret Lyon?"

Instead of sipping the cordial, Riva tossed it back like a shot of whiskey and poured another before she sat. She didn't look at Nicki and she didn't respond.

Nicki pressed. "What's your connection to the Lyons, Maman?"

"You did not swear me in. Am I under oath?" the old woman asked sharply.

"Would it make any difference if you were?" Nicki had the oddest feeling her grandmother was hiding something. But how strange that would be. Riva Bechet made a religion of being outspoken, sometimes to the point of outrageousness.

"You are my granddaughter," Riva said, staring into the tiny ring of liquid in her glass. "You live under my roof. I think it is not too much to ask that you do this one thing simply because I ask it."

With that, Riva raised her chin and left the room, taking her liqueur and turning off the lamp as she went.

Nicki was in the dark again. Still.

SCOTT WAS SATISFIED. His belly was full, his tastebuds were happy, he'd stopped at two beers and he was in good company.

To top it off, today he'd held Nicolette Bechet in his arms and kissed her.

What more did a man need?

Toni and Tony had pulled out their musical instruments. They'd already offered him a bed for the night, even though he had no intention of becoming incapacitated from booze this time around. Still, he liked the fresh air and he liked the sounds of the swamp.

He also liked being this close to Nicki.

He toyed with fantasies. Storming her room. Ravishing her with kisses she couldn't resist or disarming her with his equally irresistible charm. They would stay up late into the night, talking. She would trust him with her secrets, be awed by his compassion and understanding. She would forget he was a Lyon.

As he liked to forget, especially when he was here.

"You're quiet." That was Michel's girlfriend, Marilou.

"Yeah," he said, "I guess I am."

"Sometimes there isn't room to get a word in edgewise in this crowd."

"I'm used to that," he said.

"That's right. You're from a big family, too."

He nodded. It would have been too hard to explain that the similarities ended with the head count.

"Well, look who's come to join us!" Marilou said suddenly.

He followed the direction of her gaze. Nicki had moved into the edge of the clearing, choos-

ing a seat on a felled tree on the opposite side of
the open fire. Her eyes were on him.

"Miss Priss almost never comes down here."
Marilou leaned closer and lowered her voice, one
outsider to another. "She's such a misfit in this
family. What do you make of her?"

He wasn't about to discuss Nicki with a
stranger. "I don't know," he said, rising. "I'll
go find out."

Marilou laughed. "Good luck."

He made his way around the back of the circle.
No one else seemed to notice his movement or
Nicki's appearance. He sat on the log beside her
and knew from the way she stiffened that he was
closer than she was comfortable with. He didn't
speak right away and neither did she. The music
was starting up, but without amplifiers or microphones, it didn't interfere with conversation here
on the edge of the clearing.

"Want to dance?" he asked.

"I'll do it. I'll find your aunt."

He liked the certainty of her words. He liked
it because he wanted Aunt Margaret found. He
liked it because her self-assurance in this area
made it easier to accept her lack of it in more
personal areas.

"Thank you. I'll produce your video."

"I'll produce it," she corrected him. "You're the cameraman."

"You don't know anything about producing."

"I know what I want to accomplish."

"And what is that? Where does this compulsion to find people come from, Nicki?"

She turned to stone beside him. "I'm sure it's hard for a Lyon to understand a desire to help others. But for some of us, it's that simple."

"Is it?"

She didn't reply.

"Okay, let me help you." He reached sideways to extend his hand in front of her. "Partners?"

She ignored his hand. "One condition."

He smiled. "Only one?"

"Partners," she said, "not playmates."

He considered her condition. Then he stood up, took one of her hands and pulled her to her feet. He pulled her close and led her into a rhythm with the music.

"I said—"

"Dance partners," he said.

Her body felt right in his arms. Her hair brushed his cheek. He remembered the taste of her lips and had to battle his arousal.

"But not playmates," she reiterated.

They finished the dance. She never really relaxed in his arms. But she also never seemed to notice he hadn't made any promises.

CHAPTER SIX

SCOTT HAD NEVER BEEN one for fooling himself, but right now doing so was working out just fine.

He sat in one of the rough-hewn dining chairs on the terrace at Cachette en Bayou, soaking up the morning and allowing himself to believe that this was his new life.

He had officially turned in his resignation at WDIX-TV three days earlier; his livelihood, for the moment, was freelance video production, although he'd actually spent more time helping his neighbor, Donnie, who coordinated volunteer work for a number of social-service agencies throughout the city. This morning, after three days of dishing up gumbo at the soup kitchen, instead of returning phone calls to his family, he'd made another decision. He had stuffed a backpack full of jeans and T-shirts, locked his apartment and left a brief, vague note for Donnie. He would take the Bechet cousins up on their open-ended invitation.

His home, for now, was the cabin a few hundred yards from here, where anyone was welcome to crash at any time. He considered the Bechets his family.

He sipped his coffee and listened to the soft noises coming from the swamp. He made room for Milo the dog in his chair. He contemplated one final croissant from the batch T-John had made before he left for New Iberia this morning. He would miss T-John, although he thought he might enjoy slipping into the real bed T-John had vacated at the cabin.

Yes, life at Cachette en Bayou was good.

He let the croissant melt in his mouth.

The screen door behind him opened and closed. Some of his relaxation evaporated. He knew who had exited the house, knew it from the way the humid air suddenly filled with electricity.

Even Milo opened one eye and cocked one ear.

Nicki. Another of his areas of denial, he supposed. He again toyed with fantasies, imagining that he could wear her down, that she would eventually succumb to his charm and he would save her from the dark netherworld of her unresolved inner conflicts. Hey, it always happened that way in the movies. He might as well enjoy the fantasy, anyway.

"Any luck?" he asked.

She sat across from him and shook her head. Her hair was loose, still damp from a shower. Her overalls were fresh, not a splatter of paint anywhere. He remembered the first time he'd seen her, in a crisp suit, her hair willed into obedience. Apparently it was possible to change everything about yourself under the spell of the bayou.

"Has anyone checked on the Hollanders?" she asked, pouring another cup of coffee from the pot on the table. "Margaret Hollander Lyon. There must be some Hollanders left. Who are they? *Where* are they? Maybe they know something."

Nicki started every day by hunching over her computer, feeding it information, searching databases for any clue to his aunt's whereabouts. She knew as many tricks as any private detective. In fact, she'd told him, she'd learned all her tricks from a PI who worked for the law firm where she'd practiced briefly. She'd solved more than sixty cases of missing people during the past four years.

So far she was coming up empty-handed in her search for Aunt Margaret.

Scott rubbed his forehead. "The Hollanders? I don't remember much about them. Her father died more than fifty years ago. Before the television station was started. I learned that from the family-history feature my cousin Leslie did for the station's golden anniversary this summer.''

"A family history? Someone wrote a family history?"

He saw the spark of interest in her crystal-blue eyes; he stirred in response to that spark. "That's right. Her mother, now, I think she died sometime in the fifties. And I don't think she had any brothers or sisters.''

"I want to see that family history.''

"I don't think you'll find it much use. But we can get it.''

"Good. Maybe we'll find a disgruntled fourth cousin seven times removed, who always thought cousin Margaret should have been more generous.''

"But that seems to imply there was some kind of...'' Scott hesitated.

"Foul play is certainly a possibility. Nothing else is panning out.''

"But nobody's asked for ransom.'' He had heard through the family grapevine that someone had been draining Aunt Margaret's personal checking account in the early weeks after her disappearance. His young niece, Teresa, said talk at her house was that Crystal Jardin Tanner, one of Margaret's nieces, her trusted personal accountant and a protégé of hers to boot, had been skimming money. He'd also heard a rumor that she'd tried to throw everybody off by saying she'd had a call from Margaret. But when he talked to Crystal, it was clear that the mysterious call had upset her terribly.

Scott knew Crystal and he didn't believe for a single second that his cousin was involved in Margaret's disappearance. But it was precisely the kind of snide gossip his side of the family reveled in.

"Are you sure there's been no request for ransom? Maybe you don't know everything that's gone on."

"Some things are hard to keep secret, especially in a family whose business is digging them up."

"Okay. But if she disappeared on her own, why?"

Who knew? Scott had seen Aunt Margaret at Uncle Paul's funeral of course, but what with the flurry of activity surrounding the anniversary celebration in July, he'd hardly had the time for ten words with her in private since the spring.

The realization galled him.

"Her husband had just died," he said, repeating the speculation he'd heard from Margaret's grandchildren. "They were married fifty years. I guess she could've just…"

Repeating the theory made it sound so lame. Nicki looked skeptical.

"So in her grief this eighty-year-old woman goes off and leaves the only support she has and doesn't come back for…how long? Months?"

"She's seventy-seven," he said defensively.

Nicki rolled her eyes. "Okay. Okay. It still doesn't compute."

"No, it doesn't. You're sure one of your charming relatives hasn't buried her in the basement?"

Her flippant words angered him. But, to his chagrin, he realized he couldn't be one hundred percent sure she wasn't right.

"No," he conceded. "I'm not sure of anything."

He felt her gaze on him, but he couldn't meet her eyes. When she spoke, her voice was gentle, perhaps for the first time since he'd met her. "Well, that's a start."

She let the suggestion of foul play lie there between them, the way a good reporter left the silence for a hesitant interviewee to jump in and fill. Or a good lawyer, he supposed, which she must have been before taking the bench. Still, he had no intention of filling the silence with any more revelations about his family.

"Let's move on," he said. "Talk about where your documentary is going."

She was usually eager to talk about the project, but this time she hesitated for several moments before saying, "Okay, here's the rundown on who I want to interview."

She passed him a computer-generated list of names, with brief notations after each—location, occupation, how his or her situation had been resolved as a result of Nicki's work. Her preparation was comprehensive and professional. But he couldn't concentrate on the list. He kept thinking of Aunt Margaret and of his own fractured family. He was beginning to regret drawing an outsider into it.

And he began to understand how Judge Nicolette Bechet had felt when his family stuck its journalistic nose into her family two years ago.

THERE WAS VERY LITTLE that would have enticed Nicki to set foot on the premises of WDIX-TV. Not even the man at her side, Scott Lyon, as beguiling as he was.

But Nicki wanted that family history. And not just the official copy, she'd insisted to Scott. She wanted all the files, all the research that had gone into writing it. You never knew where a clue lurked, she'd said. And she'd seen in Scott's eyes that he knew she had her own personal motives for wanting to see that file.

So here she was, walking through the doors at WDIX-TV. Or, more correctly, Lyon Broadcasting, because the company headquarters also housed WDIX-AM radio, a news-and-information station with a talk-show format, and WDIX-FM, a station whose formatting swayed with the trends and was currently a sports-talk station.

Lyon Broadcasting operated out of an old warehouse on the river, skirting the French Quarter. An antique wrought-iron fence, lush with jasmine vines, separated the building from the sidewalk. Inside, the lobby was an elegant blend of marble floors and ultramodern reception console with understated antique settees, armchairs, side tables and light fixtures. The effect was dramatic. It also reeked of money.

The realization startled Nicki. She was accompanied by one of the heirs to all this wealth and power. Somehow she had forgotten that fact.

He drives a car you could sell and have enough cash to support every Bechet in Bayou Sans Fin for a year, she reminded herself.

It was worth keeping in mind.

"Scott!" The receptionist called out to them with a smile on her round motherly face. "We heard you'd left the station. I hope this means the rumor isn't true."

Nicki glanced at him, trying to contain her surprise and the thread of discomfort the woman's revelation caused.

Scott looked a little uncomfortable, too, and he didn't return Nicki's gaze. "I'm afraid it's no rumor, Ruth. I'm just here to...pick up something."

"I'm sorry to hear that. The Lyons, well, there aren't as many of them around these days, what with Mr. Lyon gone now and Gaby staying home with young Andy-Paul and, of course, Mrs. Lyon. We surely do miss her." Ruth pursed her lips. Her eyes were troubled. "André's here of course, but he's not himself."

André Lyon. That was who Scott said they would be seeing this morning, Nicki recalled. And Gaby and Andy-Paul were his wife and son. André was Scott's cousin and heir to most of the Lyon estate. He was also general manager of the station and very upset by his mother's disappearance and the dissension in the ranks, including an injunction filed by his cousins challenging the provisions of his father's will.

Scott asked about Ruth's son, a senior at Baylor University, and her husband, who was doing well after his double bypass surgery. Then he and Nicki made their way down a corridor toward a bank of offices.

"I feel like I'm down behind enemy lines," she whispered.

"We don't torture too many of our captives," he said.

"Hah. I've seen the evening news."

"You really think we had it in for you, don't you?"

"Not just me," she conceded.

"A television station has a job to do. That's all. It's nothing personal."

"It is to those of us who get caught in your crosshairs."

"You were a public official. That gives the public the right to know you."

"Not my personal life."

He looked at her with those searching eyes of his. "Maybe you're right," he said.

"I *am* right! And if you'd ever been a target, you'd know what I mean!"

A voice over her shoulder said, "There's something to what she says, Scott, wouldn't you say?"

Startled, she turned to see who'd spoken. A tall and distinguished-looking man, mid-fifties, perhaps. His dark eyes were troubled.

"André." Scott shook hands with the older man. "Good to see you."

"And you, Scott." He swung his gaze to Nicki. "Miss Bechet? My cousin mentioned your name when he called. Welcome to Lyon Broadcasting."

Old-school politeness. She offered him her hand and made equally polite replies.

"You locate missing people," he said. "That's what Scott tells me."

"Sometimes." She wanted to be noncommittal.

"Good. Good." He didn't say it as if he held out much hope. Then he turned his attention back to Scott. "Your leaving...well, it wasn't welcome news."

Scott nodded. "It was...time to move on."

Nicki wondered what had prompted Scott to leave the station. It had nothing to do with her, of course. But she was curious. Was it about his aunt? The family lawsuit? Something else?

André put a hand on his cousin's upper arm. His smile did little to dissipate the deep sadness in his eyes. "Hope you won't object if I hang on to the hope you'll change your mind. For a family business, we're growing woefully short of family these days."

There was something about that voice, the timbre of it, or maybe his choice of words. It was like the whisper of a memory in her ear. Could she have met André Lyon before? When she was on the bench perhaps? It was certainly not unlikely. What was unlikely was that she would have met one of the famous Lyons and forgotten about it.

"Now, I have the information you want," André said. "I pulled the files. They're on my desk, if you'll both come with me."

Following him, Nicki was still puzzling over where she'd seen him before. She wouldn't ask, that much was certain.

He handed her the file. He offered further help, any time, if she needed it. She studied his face again. Maybe she hadn't met him before; maybe he just reminded her of someone. But who?

A few minutes later she was glad to say goodbye to André. As soon as she was out of the building, all the uneasy feelings vanished. She smiled. *You're letting the Lyon family spook you, girl,* she told herself.

WATCHING NICKI BECHET, Scott decided, was endlessly fascinating. He had been doing it all day, and he hadn't grown bored with it yet.

She was sitting at a table in the gathering room of a bed-and-breakfast near Mobile, Alabama, poring intently over the files André had given them. They had dined on chicken and dumplings at a mom-and-pop diner a mile away, after spending half the day in a car and the other half taping an interview. Even when he'd had his camera pointed at the woman who'd located her birth mother seven months ago, Nicki had been the real object of Scott's attention. It said something about Nicki, he thought, that she was always so intensely involved with what she was doing that she never noticed how intensely involved he was with her.

There was the Nicki at Lyon Broadcasting, wary yet intrigued, taking in everything. André's presence, in particular, had seemed to intrigue her. He'd felt almost jealous at the way she'd soaked up every detail about his cousin.

Then there had been the Nicki who'd sat beside him on the trip to south Alabama. She had grown almost trancelike as they traveled, her eyes often closed, her face devoid of the tension he saw on it so often. He'd lowered the top on his car, expecting her to protest. Instead, she'd paid no attention at all as the wind whipped her hair and brought color to her cheeks.

Next came the Nicki who had interviewed Savannah Davis, a twenty-eight-year-old school teacher who had come to New Orleans a year ago in hopes of finding her mother. She'd found Nicki, who'd eventually uncovered the mystery of the woman's birth mother.

The Nicki who conducted the emotional interview with Savannah Davis ran the gamut from controlled professional to a young woman who empathized so deeply with her subject that her eyes were often red with unspilled tears. That Nicki had almost driven Scott to abandon his own professionalism, to lay down his camera and take her in his arms.

And now he was watching a Nicki totally focused on the task at hand. Almost mesmerized by the research she was doing.

Scott wasn't sure if his endless fascination was the beginning of love. He suspected it was. He remembered something he'd overheard his Uncle Paul say to André. *If you think watching the same woman over the morning paper for the next forty years sounds like being sentenced to purgatory, run like hell. If you think it sounds like a fine way to keep life interesting, you're on to something.*

Scott had been a kid at the time, maybe ten or so. He hadn't fully understood what the old man meant, but the words had never left him. Nor had the contentment in Uncle Paul's face when he looked at the woman he'd watched over the morning paper for decades. Scott had used Uncle Paul's advice more than once over the years as the impetus to get out of a relationship that was headed nowhere.

As he looked at Nicki, he thought maybe he was on to something.

She was stretching now, standing and working the tension out of her back. Not quite yawning, but close. She wore jeans and a faded Loyola University sweatshirt that did absolutely nothing to enhance her shape. It didn't matter. It was what lay beneath the packaging that really intrigued him.

Her eyes settled on him. Her expression turned to irritation.

"What are you looking at?" she asked.

"Find anything interesting?" he countered, nodding at her paperwork.

She shoveled the files into an untidy stack and crammed them back into a canvas tote. She marched over to him, pausing for a chocolate-chip cookie on a tray on the coffee table in front of the fireplace.

"Margaret Lyon was a fascinating woman," she said. "Did you know she was the real brains behind WDIX-TV?"

She bit into her cookie, waiting. He liked the way she ate it, in two big chomps, instead of dainty little bites. The way a kid would eat a cookie. He decided not to mention it, sure she'd retreat into control and decorum if he did.

"That's the legend," he said.

"No legend. It's all right there in the documents. She filed for the license and had the studios built and badgered the old fogies who thought radio was going to be king forever. While Paul Lyon was out drinking off his war memories or something."

"Uncle Paul never drank."

"Yes, according to the official family history, tied up in pretty bows for the big golden anniversary last summer. But if you read some of the background research that never made it into the official version…'' She shrugged, turned back for another cookie and said. ''I'm off to bed.''

He watched her climb the stairs, not an ounce of weariness in her step. Then she was gone, and the room, despite the fire, became a colder and darker place.

He contemplated that for a while, then went up to bed himself.

WHEN SCOTT AWOKE it was still dark. He came out of his sleep suddenly, not like most mornings when awareness gradually overtook him with the rising sun. He felt disoriented in the dark.

He heard footsteps in the hall outside his room. Another guest coming in, he supposed. He glanced at the clock. Three a.m. In New Orleans comings and goings at that time of night wouldn't have been unusual. He doubted there was much going on at this hour in Mobile, Alabama.

The footsteps were going down the stairs.

None of his business.

He heard a door creak open beneath his room. Fully awake now, he got up and peered out the window. It overlooked the back courtyard, where a wooden glider sat beneath a canopy of bare wisteria vines.

She walked across the yard and sat on the glider.

He couldn't see her face. But he could see her shoulders. They shook. She was crying.

He knew she wouldn't appreciate his comfort or his presence. He knew he should leave her to the dignity of her solitude. He knew all that.

But that didn't stop him. He crept through the shadowy house, his pulse kicking up and his nerve endings coming to attention as he exited the back door. She still sat on the glider, her knees drawn to her chest. She saw him and turned her back to him, tried to unobtrusively wipe her eyes on the sleeves of the terry-cloth robe she wore.

"Is there no way to get away from you?" she muttered.

He sat beside her. Felt her shift slightly to put some space between them. Felt his own reaction to her galloping out of control. He put an arm along the back of the glider and let his fingertips graze her shoulder. "Nobody should have to cry alone."

"I'm not crying."

He cupped her shoulder with his fingers, gave a gentle squeeze. He moved closer to her. He felt her relax ever so slightly.

"You can tell me, you know."

She gave a bitter little laugh. "Of course I can. If I want to be on the news at eleven."

He ignored the sarcasm and followed a hunch. "It's your mother, isn't it?" It made sense based on what Riva had told him about Nicki's personal agenda for this project and the gap in her family history. He'd heard about her father, but nothing about a mother. "You don't know who your mother is."

"That's absurd," she said so vehemently he knew he must've hit the mark.

"Or where she is, maybe."

She opened her mouth to protest, but a low moan was all that escaped. Tears followed, then muffled sobs. She collapsed against his chest. He held her there, cradling her in his arms, until he felt the tears subside.

"Aunt Margaret was the closest thing I ever had to a mother," he said softly.

"Stop it, Scott," she whispered. "I don't want or need sympathy." Her voice cracked.

"What I meant to say was that I had a mother. But she wasn't exactly the motherly type. Not very warm. She seemed only interested in engaging my father in battle. They never divorced, but...maybe they should have. I always figured it was my fault. I was a midlife baby. I came along and upset the applecart. I certainly never felt wanted—until Aunt Margaret started taking an interest in me.''

''I'm sorry,'' she said. ''Sometimes childhood stinks. But if you think I'm still pining over some lost...well, you can just...that's not...''

Her voice broke. He wrapped his arms around her and she didn't resist. She seemed, in fact, to burrow into his embrace.

He wanted to tell her, as she wept in his arms, that she was loved. That she would find her mother. That she hadn't been abandoned because she was lacking in any way. But he knew, although he wasn't sure how he knew, that nothing he could say would convince her of any of those things.

All he could do was try to show her through his actions that she was loved and lovable.

CHAPTER SEVEN

SCOTT WAS VIDEOTAPING Savannah Davis picking up her own daughter at day care. Nicki was no pro when it came to the technical side of video production, but she knew enough about people to recognize the loving-kindness with which Scott did his work. He wasn't intrusive, yet he managed to gain trust and to find ways to capture what was in people's hearts with his camera.

Either that, or she was a sucker for his routine.

She sat on the swing at the far edge of the daycare playground this morning, watching him work, watching the way Savannah and her daughter and the half-dozen other toddlers at the center warmed to him. He looked like a Hollywood version of the perfect father—relaxed and warm, reassuringly strong. He wore a loose New Orleans Saints sweatshirt, a ball cap rolled up and stuck in the back pocket of jeans faded just enough to say he had no pretentions. And when he had something to say to the children, he always hunkered down to their level, looked them squarely in the eye and spoke to them like adults.

Savannah's daughter certainly appreciated the treatment, throwing her arms around his neck at one point and laughing with sheer delight. The little girl had fallen under Scott's spell as easily as Nicki herself had the night before.

She remembered all too well how his sincerely delivered words had lulled her into believing he could understand, how his touch had turned her warm and receptive inside. She had longed for him. Longed to tell him about herself, longed to be close to him, longed to take what he so effortlessly offered. A connection. Emotional. Physical.

She had to be more careful.

She took off her cap, lifted her honey-colored hair from her shoulders and tucked it under the cap.

The Lyons were dangerous. She knew that. Without a doubt.

At last the taping was a wrap. Nicki got a hug from Savannah, and Scott got a hug from her daughter. Then they packed their gear and stowed it with their overnight bags in his car.

As the sports car purred down the main street toward the highway that would lead them back

to Louisiana and Bayou Sans Fin, Nicki hoped
he would then head to his home in the city. She
might be able to tolerate his company a few days
a week to do the tapings if he went back to his
own life in between and left her to hers. There
was no doubt that his presence in her life upset
her equilibrium. When he was around, she
wanted things she knew she couldn't have. Her
defenses were beginning to crumble beneath his
gentle assault.

She had to get away from him.

"We need to include your story," he said as
they slowed to a stop at the final red light on the
way out of town.

She decided to pretend she hadn't heard him.
After a moment she said, "The light's green."

"It will add a dimension of humanity to the
story," he persisted.

She retied her sneakers. They still felt too snug
and she tried again.

"It might lead to your mother."

She slammed her foot back to the floorboard
of the car. "I don't want to find my mother."

"That's a crock."

"You don't know anything about my story.
It's…there's nothing to it." She had to end this
conversation before she said something she re-

gretted. She was thinking all the wrong things. She was thinking of his way with Savannah's daughter. She was thinking of the way he held her in his arms, no questions asked.

"Your story is important, Nicki. As important as anyone else's."

She shrugged. "It's nothing. She was just a teenager. A runaway. Sixteen or so." Not sixteen or so. Sixteen exactly. As if Nicki didn't know every painful detail. "And she couldn't handle it, I guess—the responsibility. But it's not like she abandoned me, really. I mean, she left me with my father. That's…that's not the same thing."

She stared out the side window. He said nothing. She didn't dare look at him.

"A mother at her age, who could blame her?" she added, wanting him to contradict her.

"How old were you?"

"Let's drop it, Scott."

He didn't push. Funny how he seemed to know exactly when to push and when to back off. She'd never known a man like him.

"It's really none of your business, anyway," she added.

"I'm your friend. That makes it my business."

A howl of protest sounded in her heart. He was not a friend, could never be a friend. That was the last thing she wanted him to be. "You're a partner."

She heard him sigh. "Okay, I'm the producer. That makes it my business."

"You're the cameraman. I'm the producer."

"You don't know jack about producing."

"And you don't know jack about me, okay?"

His tires squealed as he made the turn onto the highway without slowing down. He punched some buttons on the CD player and the twangy whine of Hank Williams—not Junior, but the real thing—surrounded them.

"Your Cheatin' Heart," followed by "Longgone Lonesome Blues."

"No wonder he drank himself to death before he turned thirty," she commented between songs.

She should have left well enough alone.

"I know more about you than you do," he said, taking up their conversation where they'd left it earlier.

"Oh, please."

"You want me to tell you what I know?"

The very idea of listening to his impression of her was terrifying. Nobody dug around in Nicki Bechet's heart and soul. "I certainly do not."

"I didn't think so."

He sounded so smug. What in the world had

she been thinking, giving him credit for gentleness and empathy with people like Savannah? He was just another arrogant Lyon.

"What was her name?" he said hours later when they crossed the state line into Louisiana.

"Who?"

"Your mother."

"What possible difference does that make?"

"What did she look like?"

"Leave it alone, Scott." She used her most threatening voice, the one that made all the carpenters and electricians and plumbers at Cachette en Bayou cower.

Scott must have a hearing problem.

"Light hair, I'm guessing. Like yours. Slight of build, like you."

Still raw from the night before, Nicki felt her emotions taking over again. She would not have this. "You're wasting your breath," she said, knowing it was a lie. He was accomplishing exactly what he'd hoped. He was stirring her up. He must think she was awfully easy to control.

"The documentary's going to be only a half-truth if we don't tell your story," he said.

"Why am I not surprised you'd consider exploiting my personal life for the sake of sensationalizing the program." She dug in her bag for her sunglasses and slapped them on. "Well, you can forget it. I'm not part of the story."

"No, you're not. You *are* the story."

She wanted to kill him.

They drove the rest of the way in silence, except for the mournful wail of Hank Williams, who was so lonesome he could cry.

NICKI SPENT TWO HOURS alone with her computer when they reached Cachette en Bayou. Alone, not lonely, she told herself. She'd never minded being alone. Never. Frustrated with herself, with how out of control her life felt at the moment, she moved from screen to screen, determined to find some link to Margaret Hollander Lyon. She wanted this project over and done with.

Scott hadn't gone home. He was spending the night in the cabin, and it was all she could do to stay here in the house. They had a trip planned for more interviews the following day. She could already see him wearing another sweatshirt, another pair of jeans, another smile that took her breath away. Maybe she should get someone else to finish the interviews for the documentary. There would be more children at tomorrow's taping; he was wonderful with them. How often had she said children knew instinctively whom they could trust? Okay, so she was wrong about that, too.

She hated him. That was all there was to it.

She hated herself.

She shut down the computer, no closer to finding Margaret Lyon than she had been two hours earlier.

She wandered out to the kitchen for a banana or an apple and a cup of mint tea. She was tired. She had hardly slept the night before. That was her problem. A good night's sleep and things would look a lot better in the morning.

Riva sat in one of the kitchen chairs, feeding pieces of a hush puppy to the cats. The room vibrated with their collective purring.

"You'll make them fat," Nicki said, putting water into the copper kettle and returning it to the burner. She readied a teacup and selected an apple.

"They be old," Riva said, pinching off another piece of hush puppy. "They deserve spoiling. How is it going, your video?"

"Fine."

"Fine? What does that mean?"

"It means fine." She would *not* let her irritation show. "It means we interviewed Savannah Davis."

"And next?"

She started peeling her apple. "Next I don't know."

"And Margaret Lyon. You make progress with Mrs. Lyon?"

She peeled in short jerky motions. "Not much."

"And Scott Lyon. Your relationship with him. How does that progress?"

Nicki fumbled, dropping the knife onto the counter. She stared at her half-peeled apple and said, "I don't have a relationship with Scott Lyon."

"No?"

Riva had that same smug tone Scott had, the one that claimed to know more about Nicki than Nicki knew herself. "Absolutely not."

"Not even a kiss?"

At the reminder Nicki felt the single kiss they'd shared pour through her all over again. The kettle whistled, startling her. Setting aside her apple, she turned to the stove and poured hot water over the teabag in her cup. Her grandmother was a meddling old woman, and Nicki had no intention of having this kind of conversation with her. She cast about for a distraction.

"I went to Lyon Broadcasting yesterday on the

way out of town," she said. "I met André Lyon."

She turned in time to see her grandmother freeze momentarily, a crumb of hush puppy poised to toss to the expectant cats.

"Oh?"

The lack of interest in Riva's voice didn't match the way her body had reacted to the mention of Lyon Broadcasting and its general manager.

"He was familiar-looking. I decided I must have met him before."

Riva stood, brushed the crumbs from her fingers and shooed the cats away. "How interesting. You will excuse an old lady if she retires."

The ease with which she'd distracted her grandmother puzzled Nicki. "Have you ever met him, Maman?"

Riva was at the kitchen door. Nicki could only see her back. Once again she seemed to freeze.

"Why, maybe I have," she said. Too casually, Nicki thought.

"When?" she asked.

"Long ago, I am thinking."

"When?" Nicki pressed.

Riva shook her head. "Old women have old

memories," she said. "Cannot be trusted to remember things straight, you know."

Riva walked away. Nicki set her teacup on the counter and followed her grandmother into the hallway.

"Maman, your memory is sharp. If you ever met any of the Lyons, you'd remember it."

"I am more than eighty years, *chère fille*. Wait till you are so old, then tell me how sharp memories can be."

She started her laborious climb up the stairs, the cats at her heels. Nicki was left with no doubt that their conversation was over.

She went back to her tea and her half-peeled apple. It looked distinctly unappetizing. One cat remained, Kiku, an old Burmese who couldn't climb the stairs any longer. She slept beside the stove, curled up on a pallet Riva had made from an old quilt. Kiku eyed Nicki briefly, then lowered her head and slept.

Nicki was alone. Again. She poured out the rest of her tea and pitched the apple into the can beneath the sink. She stared out the back window, longing for…something she couldn't have. The darkness was so complete she couldn't see to the pier. Certainly not to the cabin where at least one cure for her loneliness lay sleeping.

A very foolish cure, she reminded herself.

She went up to bed.

AT BEDTIME every single night Riva prayed for each of her children and each of her grandchildren, and now her great-granddaughter.

She started with her son David because, even though he was no longer of this world, she still feared that his soul was troubled and might not yet have made it to heaven. That was her fault of course, for she had not loved him the way she should have loved him, and the lack had driven him to drugs and dissolution. So she prayed for him.

She then prayed for Simone, who had everything a woman could want in this lifetime and still was not content. Riva understood that, and feared it was her fault, as well.

She also prayed for James, her baby; for the newest member of the family, Beau's little girl; and for each and every grandchild; especially Nicolette, who felt she had been so wronged. Just as David had felt so wronged. Both had good reason to feel that way.

And finally she prayed for one whose name she never used, not even in her prayers. Her firstborn, her oldest son. The one she had given away because she believed it best.

Her grief and her guilt had gentled over the years. But tonight both emotions pierced her sharply.

So she prayed for herself, because she could see now that her decision all those years ago had had repercussions. In giving away her firstborn, she had never been able to fully enjoy the three other children God had seen fit to bless her with. Her grief had driven her, had made her wild with the need to break out of her life. She had been a bad mother, spending months at a time in the Quarter, living the life of a hedonist and a Bohemian because that was the only way to escape the empty spot in her heart where her first son should have been.

Her mistakes haunted her still.

And now, she thought as she rose from her old stiff knees, she had made another tragic mistake in bringing the two families together again.

NICKI ALWAYS PAID attention. She always knew where she was and what was happening around her. She never relinquished control.

Unfortunately the one time she didn't pay attention, she ended up exactly where she didn't want to be.

She'd dozed off in the car to one of Scott's country-music tunes. The last time she looked, they were on their way to Weyanoke, Louisiana, where one of the missing fathers she'd found now lived with his granddaughter and her two children. In the light of day her fears from the night before had seemed silly. What harm could come from doing the job they'd agreed to do? The day she wasn't a match for the appeal of a smooth talker like Scott Lyon, well...

She opened her eyes as the car slowed to a crawl, just in time to catch sight of the town-limit sign.

Welcome to Lawndale, Mississippi.

She shot upright in her seat.

Lawndale, Mississippi, her mother's home-town.

"What are we doing here?" she demanded, raking a hand through her hair.

"You're pretty smart," he said. "I think you can figure it out."

He'd been talking to Maman Riva again obviously. What incurable busybodies! Nicki looked around her as the first buildings of the town came into view. She felt the urgent need to run. And she was angry at herself for once again underestimating his arrogance. "Turn around."

The sports car continued to snake down the main street of Lawndale. People noticed them.

"I said—"

"I heard you."

Panic fluttered at the base of Nicki's throat. Although she'd been to Lawndale, Mississippi, only once in her life, Nicki found the two blocks of the main drag disturbingly familiar. There was Kasey's IGA, a hole-in-the-wall drugstore, the diner that was open for breakfast and lunch six days a week, a hardware that had more pickup trucks out front than any other business in town. And, of course, the filling station where the Greyhound bus had dropped her off twenty years ago when she'd come in search of her long-lost mother.

Not much had changed since Nicki's original pilgrimage to Debra Brackett's hometown. Except Nicki herself, who had come here the first time with a heart full of optimism, believing that once she found her mother, she would have a normal life.

She no longer had such optimism. She was content to play the hand she'd been dealt. She, Nicolette Bechet, was no longer a dreamer.

"You have no right to do this," she growled.

The sports car slid into a vacant parking spot along the street. The few pedestrians out and about on a Wednesday morning in Lawndale were curious about the two strangers in the fancy car. Nicki felt the weight of their gazes.

It crossed her mind that someone might recognize her. That she might look so much like Debra Brackett that someone would exclaim over her, "Why, miss, you're the spitting image…" or "I knew the minute I saw you that you had to be…"

It didn't happen of course.

"Let's ask around," Scott said. "That's all. See what we can find out."

"No!"

But even as she protested, she began to entertain the possibilities.

The last time she'd been to Lawndale, she'd been too young to know what questions to ask or who to ask them of. She'd come away empty-handed, quickly passed back to her father by the local authorities.

Nobody in Lawndale in 1979 would tell her a thing about Debra Brackett or her family.

Twenty years later, who knew?

With trembling hands she opened the car door

and stepped out onto the street. She looked around, suddenly hungry for a face that might belong to a cousin, an aunt, an uncle. Now that she was here, could she actually walk away without finding out?

Scott came up beside her. "Just a few questions," he said softly. "As long as we're here."

Instinctively she took the hand he offered and clutched it tightly. "As long as we're here," she repeated.

Having Scott Lyon beside her should not have been a comfort. But it was.

CHAPTER EIGHT

MOST MORNINGS, Debra Brackett Minor had to make a conscious effort to remember what town she was waking up in.

She sometimes thought that during her fifty-one years she'd lived in every hole-in-the-wall Southern town that had ever been incorporated. She'd pulled through fast-food drive-through places in Warm Springs, Georgia, and York, South Carolina. She'd rented mobile homes in Belmont, North Carolina, and Foxtail, Virginia. She'd had equally short-term relationships in Oneonta, Alabama, and Ooltewah, Tennessee, with men whose names were harder to remember than those of the towns. She'd done manicures in Mississippi and cleaned motel rooms in Florida.

Most of her hopping around had been an effort to get away from a man who was too drunk, too abusive or too shiftless. Sometimes all three.

She was tired of everything. Tired of moving around, tired of meaningless jobs, tired of men, tired of hoping that the next town—or the next man—would be the one that finally made her happy.

This morning, eyes still puffy and voice still early-morning raspy, she ordered her coffee at the Divine Donut Hut in Whispering Pines, Arkansas, population 2,907. She had awoken in an apartment over a garage, instead of a mobile home, and she wasn't sharing a bed with some sorry drifter who couldn't stick with a job any better than he could stick with a woman. She supposed, as she forked over her ninety-seven cents, that the job she was headed to was less glamorous than gluing acrylic nails onto the fingers of some woman trying to impress her man.

But for the first time, Debra was content to be exactly where she was, doing exactly what she was doing.

That might not sound like much for some folks, but for Debra it felt pretty good. After years of being down on herself for the mess she'd made of her life, after years of missing the only kid she'd ever had, Debra felt almost at peace with herself. Sure, she still regretted all those lousy relationships and the daughter she'd been too young to take care of herself. There were still days when she thought about Nicolette and wished she had the courage to walk into her girl's fancy office in that New Orleans courthouse. That had been the clincher of course. Finding out that her baby was a judge. A judge didn't need some no-account loser turning up on her doorstep, messing up the good life she'd made for herself. No, Debra had made her own bed and was resigned to lying in it.

She pulled into the parking lot of the cinderblock nursing home. It was barely daylight, but the coffee had given her the boost she needed. She swung through the back door with a big smile for the night crew.

"Hey, Bradley," she said, the way she always did.

Bradley gave her the end-of-shift smile he always gave her. But this morning he said, "Hey, Deb, how come you've always got such a big smile first thing in the morning?"

She started to laugh it off, but changed her mind. "You know, Bradley, I was just thinking about that on the way over here. Truth is, in a few minutes, I'll be doing something I really like doing."

"Emptying bedpans?"

She chuckled. "More'n that. I'll be making

life a little brighter for a bunch of old folks who
don't have much that's good in their lives.''

''You can say that again. This place is a dump,
no question.''

Debra had figured out right away that most of
the people who lived here now hadn't had easy
or pampered lives. And old age wasn't being any
better to them. ''That's where I come in. I've got
the power to make things a little better for
them.''

Bradley looked skeptical. And as she went on
her way, Debra figured he wouldn't understand,
anyway. All she did, apart from emptying bedpans, was fluff up their pillows and rub lotion on
their backs and help them change into clean
nightgowns. She chatted away to them—even the
ones who didn't understand a blessed thing she
said. Sometimes they smiled at her. She couldn't
have explained why, but whenever that happened, it made her day. Filled the emptiness in
her heart.

Of course, the work was hard, too. Some of
the old people were in awful shape and a lot of
them weren't in their right mind. But Debra liked
thinking of herself as a guardian angel, sent to a
wretched place like Whispering Pines Nursing
Home to make their last days as good as possible.

And to top it all off, she got to wear a crisp white uniform and those squishy nurse's shoes. No matter how long she was on her feet, they never hurt.

She checked her roster for the day. Time for room 19's bath. Mrs. Margie Paul. Mrs. Paul was one of Debra's favorites, even though the old dear barely knew what planet she was on. She was always babbling about things that made no sense. Lions, for example. Debra supposed she was having nightmares.

"Good morning, Mrs. Paul," she said cheerfully, although she could tell right away that the old woman was agitated again this morning. "How about a nice bath and a fresh gown for you today?"

Mrs. Paul groaned and thrashed. She shoved Debra's hands away. "Lyon," she said. "Not Paul. Husband. Lyon."

Debra chuckled and continued preparing the old woman for her bath, despite the struggles and protests. "Yeah, I know. My husband was kind of a bear, himself. Men can be that way. That's why I dumped him."

Mrs. Paul whimpered.

Debra didn't think Mrs. Paul had dumped her husband. She noticed the faint indentation on the ring finger of her left hand where the old woman had obviously worn a wedding ring for many years. Debra wondered what had happened to the ring. Maybe her family had it. Maybe someone at Whispering Pines had it. That wouldn't be surprising.

Debra found the pills then, under the edge of the pillow. She found them many mornings and made a point to get them down the patient without alerting the nursing crew. Sighing, she murmured, "Mrs. Paul, you have to take your medicine. If they find out you're spitting it out, they'll hook you up to an IV. Needles in your arm. Now, you don't want that, do you?"

Mrs. Paul looked at her with pleading in her eyes. "No," she said, her voice barely audible. "Not medicine. Not!"

Debra soothed the old woman, brushing her forehead until Mrs. Paul relaxed. What she didn't like to say, even to an old woman who couldn't possibly understand her, was that patients who created problems were often neglected at Whispering Pines. Neglected, or worse.

Debra wouldn't let that happen to Mrs. Paul or any of her patients, not if she could help it.

"There, there," she said. "Let's not make a

fuss, Mrs. Paul. Open up and take your medicine.''

Mrs. Paul was sleeping peacefully when Debra left. She didn't know exactly what was wrong with the poor old woman, who never had visitors or even callers. But she knew that sleep was the best thing for her. It made Debra feel better knowing that Mrs. Paul was no longer agitated, the way she'd been when Debra first came on duty.

LAWNDALE, MISSISSIPPI, was an exercise in frustration and heartache.

Buster Ranlo, who worked in the feed-and-seed department at Lawndale Hardware, remembered Debra Brackett. Buster had a well-tended comb-over and a potbelly and a gleam in his eye that surfaced when they asked about Nicki's mother.

"Sure, I remember Debbie," he said, his husky voice growing a little softer.

Nicki's heart clutched. How long had it been since she'd spoken to someone who knew her mother? Aside from Maman Riva of course, and Aunt Simone or Uncle James, and none of them had much to say about Nicki's mother. Her fingers automatically tightened around Scott's. He gave her hand a squeeze. She forced words out around the knot in her throat. "You do?"

"Sure. Went to high school with her. Before she took off, that is. We was all set to go to the junior-senior prom together. She was only a sophomore, but I was a junior, so she was going with me. But she took off before we finished out the school year."

The words roared in Nicki's ears. *She took off.* Her mother had a habit of taking off apparently. "Why did she leave?"

Buster shook his head. "Wish to goodness I knew. That girl broke my heart, leaving like that. Had my tuxedo rented, the whole nine yards."

Nicki had a hard time imagining Buster Ranlo as a high-school junior in a rented tuxedo. But not as hard a time as she had imagining her mother living in this town and agreeing to go with him to the prom.

"What was she like?"

Buster chuckled. "Honey, she was as sweet as anybody you ever knew."

"Sweet?" Nicki tried not to be disappointed, tried not to think about how much she'd wanted to hear things that would make her feel connected to her mother. Like independent, tough-minded, things Nicki would recognize in herself.

"Sure. You know, never a cross word for any-body, always trying to make everybody happy. Tell you what, I woulda been a lot better off all these years if I'd married Debbie, instead of who I did."

So much for the psychological gene pool.

They talked to a junior-high teacher, who said that Debra Brackett hadn't had much affinity for things educational. They were directed to the re-tired man who sold white lightning back in the days when liquor couldn't be purchased legally in Lawndale and learned that Debra's father had been one of his most loyal customers. They talked to the woman who had lived next door to the Bracketts for twenty-six years and remem-bered only that the Bracketts kept to themselves, weren't very neighborly and were therefore little missed when they unexpectedly moved in the early 1970s.

"Do you remember where they went?" Nicki asked.

"Why, no. It was none of my business."

They found Debra's best friend, Nancy Felton, who now owned and operated The Best Little Hairhouse in Lawndale. A tired-looking woman who could have used the services of the beauty shop herself, Nancy Felton was leery of answering questions at first.

"Who are you, anyhow?" Nancy asked Nicki, squirting permanent-wave solution onto the tightly wound hair of a woman who looked uneasy about having strangers witness her transformation.

"I…" Nicki glanced at Scott. He gave her an encouraging smile. He'd been by her side all morning, passing no judgment, simply being supportive. And he hadn't once mentioned dragging out the video camera. He seemed content simply to accompany her on her search.

"Bless my soul, I know who you are!"

Nancy Felton's exclamation startled Nicki and drew the stares of everyone in the salon. Nancy's eyes were wide; she pressed her fingers to her lips. From the way she wrinkled her nose, those fingers reminded her of the permanent-wave solution she was in the process of applying.

"Oh, Lordy, let me finish up with Darlene here and we'll have us a cup of coffee. Y'all set down over yonder and I'll be right with you." She looked at Nicki one more time, murmured, "Bless my soul," and turned back to Darlene's head.

Nicki and Scott walked to the vinyl sofa beside

the front door. Nicki was acutely aware of the attention on her now. "Maybe we should go."

Scott took her hand and pulled her down onto the sofa. "Let's see what she has to say."

"But—"

"You'll regret it forever if you walk out now," Scott said.

His voice was very reassuring. She had the most disturbing feeling that she was beginning to trust Scott Lyon. To like him, even, which was worse than simply wanting him.

"Maybe I'll regret it if I don't."

"You'll never convince me you'd rather walk away from the truth than face it," he said.

They shared a look. She wanted to avert her eyes, but his commanded her honesty and she held his gaze. He did know her, the way he kept claiming. She ached with the need to be enveloped in his embrace.

Nancy joined them in five minutes, wiping her hands on the pink towel tucked into the front of her jeans. She was a large woman with an open face. And she couldn't seem to take her eyes off Nicki.

"Lordy, I can't believe I didn't see it right off," she said. "You've got to be Debbie's girl."

Nicki's mouth went dry. "Yes. I...I'm Nicki. Nicolette."

Nancy sat in a chair that matched the couch and smiled at them. "Well, I declare, ain't this something. I'd heard Debbie had a little girl of course. But, well, you never know. People say most anything. You can't believe half of what you hear."

Nicki's heart sank. "Then you haven't talked to her?"

"To Debbie? No, no, I haven't. She left here our sophomore year in high school and never set foot in Lawndale again, as far as I know. 'Course, that didn't surprise me one bit."

"It didn't?"

"No. Debbie hated this little town and near 'bout everybody in it. They all looked down on her, you know. As pretty and smart as she was, they all looked right down their noses at her."

"She was smart?"

"That girl read every book in the public library before she hit high school, I swear she did. She knew everything."

"But her teacher said—"

Nancy waved a chapped hand. "Oh, them. Debbie never opened her mouth in class. And they all thought, just because of her family, you know, that she wasn't too bright.''

"Because of her family?''

"Because of the drinking.'' Nancy cocked her head to one side. "Honey, what're you doing here asking questions about your mama, anyway?''

"I... I was hoping somebody might know where she is.''

Nancy looked dumbfounded. "You mean she's lost?''

"Well, I—''

"How long's it been since you've seen your mama, Nicolette?''

Nicki hesitated. Maybe it was something in the air in Lawndale, Mississippi, but she trusted this woman, too. "I was four when she left.''

Nancy sagged back in her chair. "Sakes alive! You mean to tell me Debbie Brackett walked out on her little girl? I swear, I just can't feature it.''

Somehow the woman's astonishment made Nicki feel inadequate. Clearly Debra Brackett's best friend believed she didn't have it in her to walk out on her daughter. The only answer to the riddle was that her daughter had been lacking. Nicki had sat in on enough family-court hearings to know that the reasons for abandoning a child were complex and rarely had anything to do with the child. But the feelings buried deep inside her had little to do with what her professional experience told her.

She wasn't good enough. She'd always felt it deep in her bones.

She had to change the direction of this conversation, get the focus off an abandoned four-year-old.

"So you don't know where she is? Where she might have been all these years?"

Nancy laughed softly and a little sadly. "If I knew where she was, I'd have gone after her myself. She left here with seventy-five dollars out of my piggy bank. Borrowed it, she said. No, hon, I've heard things over the years of course, but nothing for sure."

"What kind of things?"

"Oh, you know. She got married in Georgia. I don't reckon that was your daddy, was it?"

Nicki shook her head.

"Good. I heard he was a mean son of a gun."

Nicki's emotions were in turmoil, her heart ready to burst in her chest. *A mean son of a gun.* Had her mother been abused? Had she had another child? Did she, Nicki, have a half sister or brother?

"What was her husband's name?" Nicki's dry lips would barely form the words.

"Minor. Eddie Minor. They were somewhere in Georgia…oh, someplace with a hot springs." She paused and pressed a finger to her forehead. "I think it was called Warm Springs."

Nicki's pulse gave an extra beat. Not Miller or Milner, as she'd thought, but Minor. Now she had a town and a name. They were the first real clues she'd had in years.

Nancy went on. "Then I heard she was down in Florida somewhere. After that, her folks took off, too, and I never heard anything else from her." She shook her head. "I sure did hate that, too. We were close once. Real close. I think I was the only one she ever really talked to." Nancy checked her watch. "Listen, hon, I've got to rinse that solution off Darlene's curlers before she kinks up like a Brillo pad. Say, if you find out anything about Debbie, tell her Nancy wants her seventy-five dollars back, okay? Tell her I won't even charge her interest."

Nicki smiled. "I'll tell her," she said, trying not to rest too much hope on the name of a man and a town. But she'd done this kind of search often enough to know that sometimes one break was all that was necessary to unlock everything.

Debra Brackett Minor. She had a lead.

NICKI KEPT A TIGHT LID on her excitement all the way back to Bayou Sans Fin.

It wasn't that she didn't want to share her feelings with Scott. It wasn't even that she didn't trust him to understand and respect what was going on inside her. Because she did. It was more a case of not trusting fate. If she let the universe, including Scott, know how optimistic she felt, might not all of it be snatched away?

"Will any of that help you?" Scott had asked as soon as they'd left The Best Little Hairhouse. "Having a last name? A town in Georgia?"

"Maybe."

He faced her over the top of the car as they were getting in. His eyes searched her face in a way that made her feel defenseless. He could see way more than she wanted him to see, she was certain. Usually she could compose herself so well that no one could see beneath her mask. Except perhaps Maman Riva.

And now Scott.

He invited her to the cabin once they reached Cachette en Bayou, as if the little two-room fishing shanty belonged to him. It was empty this week, the cousins scattered—T-John back to his restaurant in New Iberia, Tony and Toni on a brief road trip with their band, Beau and his wife visiting her relatives, Michel sniffing after a new lady friend who had no intention whatsoever of staying in the musty little cabin.

Nicki went with him under the pretext of planning the next day's shoot.

But in truth she went because she wanted to be with him.

They left the door open, allowing the bayou in with its scents and sounds. She sat, knees drawn up under her chin, on a narrow cot that served as sofa and bed. Scott lounged on a matching cot at a right angle to hers, legs splayed. He looked so relaxed. She envied him that.

"You're excited," he said. "About talking to your mother's friend."

She tried to deny it, but the lie wouldn't come. "What makes you think that?"

He smiled softly. "Your eyes have fire in them."

She blinked.

"You can hide a lot, but you can't hide that."

She shrugged dismissively and reached for the notebook beside her feet. Time to get back to work. He reached it with his foot first, nudging it beyond her reach.

"Forget tomorrow," he said.

"But—"

"If you trusted life, what would you do to-night?"

The uncanny way his words echoed her earlier thoughts startled her. She wanted to jump up and leave, but she was tired of running from him and whatever it was he kept trying to force on her.

"What makes you think I don't trust life?"

"I see that in your eyes, too."

He leaned forward, elbows on his knees. She had an urge to inch back, although he was certainly still a safe distance away. Sometimes she felt there was no safe distance from Scott Lyon.

"Life doesn't treat anybody with kid gloves, Nicki."

The soft way he spoke her name took the sting out of his pronouncement. It left her feeling naked before him, stripped of all her defenses.

"Never?" she asked in a whisper.

He shook his head. "If it was all a piece of cake, we could get through it alone. We'd never reach out. Never connect."

"So?"

His hand came closer, grazed the side of her face. "So that's why we're put here. To connect."

She didn't want to let herself believe it. "A nice philosophy," she said with as much cynicism as she could muster.

"Don't do that."

She opened her mouth for a sharp retort, but his eyes stopped her. Silver, with no darkness in them, no shadows, no hiding places. She'd never seen eyes so open. They invited her in. She moved toward him and found herself too close.

"Leave me alone," she whispered, but realized too late that the words did not match her tone.

"I can't do that," he said, his words a whisper against her lips.

"I don't want to connect," she said. "Not with you."

"Not wanting to is different from being afraid to." He spoke as gently as he took her in his arms. He pressed her lightly to his chest, her thighs touching his, his fingertips fluttering over her back. She felt warm wherever they touched, warm and energized.

"I'm not afraid," she said.

"Yes, you are."

Of course she was. Terrified. Everyone she'd ever wanted, needed, loved, had left her, walked out, abandoned her. And she had allowed that single fact to rule her life.

Then she forgot the fear, lost it in the meeting of their lips and the sudden urgency of her body pressed to his. She felt his chest beneath her palms, solid and warm, the beat of his heart moving through her, into her. She felt his arms, drawing her closer, enfolding her, supporting her. She felt his lips, opening her. She was filled with him from the inside out before she understood what was happening.

It felt right.

Not risky or frightening. Just so right.

Glad she wasn't wearing a bra, she lifted her sweater over her head, then ran her fingers beneath his T-shirt. A smattering of crisp curls caught her fingertips. His soft groan trembled against her lips. She rolled his shirt up, pressed her bare breasts to his chest.

He gripped her upper arms, pulled back from her lips and looked down into her eyes. She saw the question in his eyes.

"Don't ask me if I'm sure," she said. "That would be asking too much."

He hesitated, but only for an instant. Then he met her lips.

The closer he came, the more her fear receded. The more she revealed to him, the more real she felt to herself. And she knew, as he stared deeply into her eyes and joined their bodies, that her defenses had crumbled completely.

CHAPTER NINE

SHE SLEPT THE WAY his young cousin, Andy-Paul, slept—soundly, without moving, the sleep of someone at peace.

Scott hadn't expected that. He had been prepared for her wariness to kick in the moment they completed their lovemaking. He'd even told himself not to be surprised if she insisted on going back to the big house, where she could sleep in her own bed, alone and undisturbed.

Instead, she had fallen into a deep sleep, curled against his belly, fist under her cheek. As sweet as a child. He smiled, doubting she would care for his comparison.

He lay beside her for a long time, listening to the whisper of her breath, learning the pattern of delicate blue veins on her eyelids and the curve of her hip draped by the worn quilt he'd pulled over her. He grew aroused all over again, remembering the silken texture of her skin, the feel of taut muscle as their bodies strained for release.

He allowed his palm to float over the strands of her hair—some gold, some moonlight silver and some touched by honey. Complex, like the rest of her.

His fascination for her had changed throughout the day just passed. He had started out wanting her, longing for her, hoping to break through her barriers and find the woman he believed to be hidden there. As he'd followed her around Lawndale, studied her while she talked to people who had known her mother, he'd seen the barriers fall even as she believed they remained in place. He'd seen the layers of bitterness and cynicism give way to hope.

And as the layers peeled away, he'd taken the final irrevocable plunge into love for the woman he discovered beneath the facade.

Someday she might be ready to hear that he loved her. But not yet. She was still too skittish.

He stayed beside her on the narrow cot as long as he could, thinking she might wake up. But she didn't, and eventually stiff muscles and an empty belly dragged him out of the cot, into some clothes and up to the big house. The lights downstairs were still on, so perhaps Riva was still up. Besides, he knew from his previous stays that the young Bechets often made midnight treks to the house for leftovers. His presence wouldn't startle her.

In the fridge he found a covered platter of *boulette* and half a loaf of crusty French bread. Ravenous, he put together a sandwich with the bread and the crawfish meatballs, then wandered the house, wolfing it down.

With his photographer's eye, he took in the artful arrangement of locally made baskets on the kitchen counter, the stack of well-thumbed cookbooks, the antique wooden coffee grinder. He stopped to stroke the cat sleeping on a quilt beside the stove, then moved into the foyer. There, the spill of light from the family room cast shadows on a rustic parson's bench where three of the family cats had settled for the night. One of them raised a suspicious eye. He leaned over to caress her silky fur and she dropped back to sleep.

He followed the light into the family room.

Riva sat in her chair, swaddled in a bright red-and-gold afghan, eyes closed, chin drooping to her chest, snoring lightly. Scott smiled, wondering if he should wake the old woman and take her up to her bed. Realizing he felt at home enough to even consider it gave him yet another lift. He belonged here; they accepted him. The sensation filled an emptiness he'd carried around for a long time.

He not only loved Nicki, he loved her home, her family, her land.

As he studied the old woman, he made himself a promise. He would make a place for himself here, no matter what it meant. He could learn to shrimp with Beau and Michel or help out Simone's family on the adjoining rice farm. He was finally home.

Content with his decision, Scott approached Riva. He noticed the book open on her lap and caught the scent of gardenia that he had come to associate with her. He smiled and leaned over to wake her with a whisper and a hand on her shoulder. As he did, something in the book on her lap caught his eye.

It was a newspaper clipping about Paul Lyon's death.

His hand paused in midair. Why in the world would Riva Bechet have a newspaper clipping about his uncle's death?

He looked more closely. The book appeared to be a scrapbook, an old one—the new clipping about Uncle Paul's death was pasted to a page that looked dingy and slightly tattered on the edges. Curious, he slipped it from beneath her hands and out of her lap. He turned back a page and saw another familiar clipping, this one of André at the WDIX-TV anniversary celebration. His astonishment growing, Scott told himself he'd stumbled onto something that was none of his business. He should put Riva's scrapbook down now. But he couldn't. He felt compelled to make sense of this. Why would she collect clippings about his family? Scott continued to flip backward through the scrapbook. Maybe the book simply catalogued the history of New Orleans and his family was incidental to that.

Every page held another clipping about the Lyon family.

He turned to the beginning of the book. The clippings went all the way back to 1943. The first was a yellow brittle one from the local paper, mentioning the christening of the youngest Lyon heir, André, born just days before his father left to cover the war in Europe, according to the paper.

Scott's fingers began to tremble. More than fifty years of his family's history was chronicled in this book. His family was famous of course, but this meticulous decades-long obsession with the Lyons startled him.

As the member of a prominent family, he'd

seen obsession before and knew it could get ugly. He remembered all too clearly a young governess who had decided she was destined to marry Alain. Nothing dissuaded her, not even dismissal. She had stalked his brother for months, had even followed young Scott to school in hopes of enlisting his help.

He remembered the desperate look in her eyes.

Shivering, Scott stared down at the sleeping woman who had first summoned him with a subterfuge.

What did she want with him? What did she want from the Lyon family? What was her interest in Aunt Margaret's disappearance?

Spooked, he quietly closed the scrapbook.

Suddenly the house, the silence, the isolation that had moments ago felt so comfortable and welcoming seemed ominous. He wanted desperately to go to Nicki, but he couldn't imagine what he would say to her, without making it sound like an accusation. His thoughts were in turmoil. Nicki would see anything he did now as a betrayal.

He had to clear his mind.

He had to get away before Riva awoke.

He left the house.

He drove for hours, the urge to return to Nicki

warring with his urge to get away from something he didn't understand and instinctively feared.

Finally, he forced himself to return to Cachette en Bayou. To Nicki. As he approached the turnoff, another thought occurred to him. What if the scrapbook wasn't Riva's at all? What if it belonged to someone else—someone who had made no secret of her bitterness toward his family.

What if the scrapbook belonged to Nicki?

He braked abruptly. He sat on the dark lane. Perspiration popped out on his upper lip. He didn't believe it, but could he afford to ignore the possibility? He backed out of the driveway and pointed his car toward New Orleans. He continued waging his inner war all the way back to the city.

The battle was still not over when he found himself back in New Orleans.

NICKI AWOKE with a start.

She was cold and she was alone and, most disconcerting of all, she was naked.

She sat up, shoving hair out of her face, and looked around her at the familiar cottage. She saw the jumble of her clothes on the floor and it came back to her.

Scott.

Unease tempered the elation in her heart. They had made love. It had been wonderful, not just physically but in the way their hearts had connected. She remembered it vividly—the exquisite moment when their bodies became one, when she breathed in rhythm with his breath, when his eyes had looked into her soul and she hadn't been too afraid to let him see.

Making love with Scott had been the most intimate act she'd shared with anyone in her entire life. But if it had been so wonderful, where was Scott?

His T-shirt and jeans were not in that pile on the floor, she noticed.

Shivering, she quickly threw on her clothes and ran her fingers through her hair. He was here somewhere. On the dock, maybe, unable to sleep. Up at the house, foraging for food. Easily explained, if she simply set aside her paranoia for five minutes. Her heart thumped uncomfortably as she left the cabin and scanned the moonlit clearing. He wasn't here, either.

Nor was he at the dock.

Lights were on at the house, however, and she

started toward it. But with every step she took, her confidence ebbed. Maybe their lovemaking had not meant as much to him. Maybe she was kidding herself.

He wasn't in the kitchen. Or the foyer. Or in the family room, where Maman Riva stirred slightly as she passed, murmuring something in her sleep. Nicki searched the entire house and found no sign of Scott. Finally she did the thing she'd been avoiding. She went out onto the porch, searched the darkness for his car, walked to the spot beneath the live oak where he'd parked earlier.

The spot was empty. Scott was gone.

The blow almost drove her to her knees.

HE CALLED HER three times the next morning. In the clear light of day, it was obvious that his family had nothing to fear from Nicki. She'd had nothing to do with luring him out to Bayou Sans Fin. He had a lot of explaining to do, a lot of apologies to make, and he planned to do whatever it would take to alleviate the pain he knew he'd caused the night before. But each time, Riva answered the phone, and he couldn't make a sound.

He tried again at lunch time. This time, he heard the voice he wanted to hear.

"Nicki, thank God, I—"

The line went dead with a resounding click in his ear.

He was a jerk. She was right to hang up on him. He'd walked out. Walked out, for God's sake! What had he been thinking?

He dialed again. This time, she answered, "Don't call here any more. Don't come here any more."

"Wait, Nicki. Let me—"

She hung up again.

"—explain."

He knew then he was going to have to drive out to Cachette en Bayou. Maybe it was best that way anyway. He could ask Riva about what he'd seen. Get some explanation. Then he wouldn't have to carry around this nagging notion that he needed to tell his family about the old woman's interest in them.

He'd been trying to set things right for a week, the worst week of his life. He'd driven out, all right, but it was useless. Nicki refused to see him. Refused to hear his explanation, his apology, anything. He sent e-mail, flowers, a letter by snail mail, which would probably come back unopened any day now. He told himself to give her time. He told himself it would all blow over. He told himself he'd overreacted and he would find a way to make it up to her.

Now, he was topping off the worst week of his life with a visit to Lyoncrest. His feet dragged as he approached the family home. A standout even in the city's elegant Garden District, Lyoncrest glittered tonight. Antique chandeliers sparkled behind every leaded-glass window, multiplying their shimmer. French doors were opened onto every gallery on all three stories of the 1830s mansion, enhancing the impression of hospitality and celebration.

Scott knew he would be welcome here, but his heart wasn't in the visit. Seeing his family, he knew, would stir up all his conflicted feelings over what he knew about Riva Bechet. Should he tell them? He'd resisted the idea all week, knowing what it would do to Nicki. But seeing the family, wondering if he held information that might lead to Aunt Margaret…

At the best of times, coming to Lyoncrest stirred conflicting emotions for Scott. The house had been a symbol of the rift in his family for as long as he could remember. His father, Charles, had approached each obligatory visit with a face set in rigid disapproval. And after each visit, he would retell the story of being ousted from the house when his brother, Paul, had returned from World War II. Scott and his brothers had listened raptly, soaking up the colorful tale of family betrayal.

Much later, Scott had learned from his mother that there was more to the story—his father's incompetence in running the family radio station, his desire for his own sister-in-law and his refusal to live under the same roof with his successful and popular brother. Even Charles's insistence that he'd been forced to give up his career of choice as a classical pianist was revisionist history, according to Scott's mother. Charles had never had the gumption to follow his heart, opting instead for the safety of the family business.

So Scott seldom made an appearance at Lyoncrest. It took a very special occasion. Tonight was one of those. Tonight the Lyons marked a new addition to the family. Skipper Tanner would be the latest member of the next generation; his adoption by Scott's cousin Crystal and her husband, Caleb, was final today.

Gift under his arm, fingers on the massive door knocker, Scott could only hope that the next generation would have an easier time of it than his generation or the previous one.

The party was in full swing, allowing him to slip in without much fanfare. The children—Skipper and Andy-Paul, as well as two of his own nieces and a nephew—were gathered around an antique electric train set that Scott remembered from his own childhood. And both parlors were filled with family and a handful of longtime Lyon Broadcasting employees who were widely regarded as family.

Scott should have felt right at home. What he felt was guilty. Guilty about his family. But most of all, overwhelmingly, guilty about walking out on Nicki.

"Well, if it isn't the prodigal cousin back from the swamp!"

Crystal's wry voice broke through the polite murmur of conversation. He glanced around, noted that few others in the room had even registered Crystal's comment, and turned to his cousin for a kiss on the cheek and a warm hug.

"Congratulations," he said. "Wife and mother all in a matter of months. That's a big change for my favorite workaholic."

She smiled at his gentle gibe, her eyes sweeping the room until she spotted her husband and son. "Reformed workaholic, if you don't mind. From here on out, the family comes first."

Their eyes met. Scott imagined that the brief shadow clouding her eyes was reflected in his. How many times had they heard Aunt Margaret say the same thing? *Family comes first.*

"It doesn't seem right without her," Crystal said, her voice suddenly husky.

"No," he replied, "it doesn't."

"But she'd give us both a good talking to if she caught us moping around about it," Crystal said, banishing the mood quickly. "And she'll really have your hide when she finds out you've jumped ship. What's going on, cuz?"

What, indeed?

"I got tired of all the bickering," he said.

"What's this? Tired of all the bickering?" Leslie, André's stepdaughter, approached with two champagne flutes in her hand. "I thought bickering was the Lyon legacy."

The three of them laughed as she thrust a flute at each of them.

"What happened to my shy cousin?" Scott asked. "You're more like Aunt Margaret every day."

"Marriage agrees with me apparently," Leslie said. "And I heard there's a woman behind your escape from WDIX-TV. Come on, Scotty, give."

His two cousins were not to be denied, he knew. But what could he tell them? What could he say that wouldn't condemn him? "I—"

"A gun-toting Cajun woman, that's what I

heard," Crystal interjected, one black brow arched in question.

"Vicious gossip," he said with as convincing a smile as he could muster. He doubted it was very convincing. He'd felt the color rush to his face as soon as Nicki was mentioned. If he hadn't been such a coward, she might be by his side right now.

"Tell," said Leslie, "or I'll call in Mother. Nobody holds out on Mother."

"Please," he teased back. "Not Gaby."

They played at cajoling the story out of him for the next ten minutes, and Scott played along. But the situation with Nicki and Riva kept twisting and turning in his mind, leaving him in turmoil.

Scott's endearingly pushy cousins finally released him. He soon realized that they had at least afforded him some protection from the other curious souls in the room. He found himself fending off a constant barrage of questions about his departure from WDIX-TV, including some very pointed questions from Gaby, André's wife. When Mary Boland, long-standing director of engineering at WDIX-TV, finally rescued him, Scott was grateful for the reprieve. Mary was the daughter of one of the radio station's original announcers, Red Reilley, and had practically grown up with André, so she was more like family than colleague.

"There's a spot for you in heaven," he said as he slipped to the edge of the buffet table with the older woman.

"Rescuing people when Margaret got her hands on them has been my chief responsibility at WDIX-TV for decades, you know. I'm finding it works with Gaby, also."

It was good to laugh with Mary, even about indomitable Aunt Margaret.

"It's a testimony to her, you know," Mary said when their laughter died. "That we keep talking about her as if she was here."

"I still feel her here. I guess we all do."

Mary nodded, a sheen of tears clouding her eyes. "She's touched so many people profoundly. Once your life intersects with Margaret Lyon's, you never forget."

The comment stirred another uneasy memory of the scrapbook. And it suddenly occurred to Scott that he was talking to someone who might know if Aunt Margaret had ever crossed paths with Riva Bechet. Someone who might afford him a hint of whether there was something to fear from her.

He wasn't sure he wanted to know.

"That reminds me," he said, looking into his empty champagne flute and forcing himself to plow through his hesitation. "I met someone who…who might have known Aunt Margaret from the old days. A Mrs. Bechet. Riva Bechet."

"Bechet?" Mary frowned and pursed her lips. "No, I… What did you say her given name was?"

"Riva."

"Riva. We knew a Riva once, but—"

"She might have been Riva Reynard in those days."

"Yes! That's it. Riva Reynard. Oh, my, that was a lifetime and a half ago. Did Dad ever have a few tales to tell Mom about Riva Reynard!"

Scott felt his uneasiness grow into something close to fear. "Who was she? How did she know Aunt Margaret?"

"Why, she used to work for WDIX radio back, oh, I don't know, fifty years ago or more."

Scott felt a chill seep into his blood. "She worked for us?"

"That's right. I never met her myself of course. But I remember seeing her in the Quarter once, years later, and one of the camera crew said she used to work for us, during the War maybe. Said she was sweet on Paul.''

Scott's stomach took a nosedive. ''I suppose it could be a different woman.''

''I suppose. This woman was quite a character. Very flamboyant. Artsy, I guess you'd say. Wild clothes, bright colors, that kind of thing.''

Just like the Riva Bechet who had beckoned him into her life a few weeks earlier.

''Oh, André, you remember Riva Reynard, don't you?''

Scott's mood sank further when Mary beckoned his cousin. ''The artist? Just from hearsay. She was a bit of a legend in the Quarter during the fifties, as I recall. I heard someone say once that she could be the most jovial person in the room—unless you said the wrong word. Then she'd go on quite a tear.'' He paused. ''Why? She's surely dead now.''

Scott stared at his cousin, knowing now that he definitely owed the family the information he had. There was a connection, possibly a strong link between the families. He had to do this, even knowing what it would do to the woman he had already wronged.

''Actually,'' he said, ''I met her a few weeks ago.''

André seemed to pick up on his cousin's strange mood. He looked at Scott intently. "And?"

Scott hesitated. He knew what would happen if he told André what he'd seen in the hands of an eccentric old woman who had once been sweet on Uncle Paul and famous for her tantrums. With virtually no leads in Margaret's disappearance, he would insist on telling the police. The police would insist on talking to Riva Bechet.

And Nicki's hideaway would be invaded.

How could he do that to her?

How could he withhold any information that might help them find Aunt Margaret? He was damned if he did and damned if he didn't.

He cleared his throat. "She...she has the strangest thing, André. A scrapbook. All about the Lyon family."

Mary gasped. André went white.

It was no consolation to Scott that he'd done the only thing he could. All he could think of was Nicki and the pain he was going to cause her—again.

CHAPTER TEN

NICKI LOOKED at the wallpaper swatches taped to the newly plasterboarded wall in the dining room. Shades of gold or taupe, stripes or fleur-de-lis, smooth versus textured, none of it sparking any enthusiasm in her.

"Let's just paint it nouveau-riche red, get a big old gold chandelier and call it done," said Toni, who sat Buddha-style on top of the massive cherry dining table.

"Whatever," Nicki said.

"*Mon dieu,* you are a drag these days. Go after him, for the love of Pete!"

"MYOB." Nicki's heart wasn't in her retort, either.

"What exactly happened between you two?"

Nicki snatched the swatches off the wall and tossed them into the corner with a stack of paint cans and wallpapering supplies. What exactly happened between them was what she'd been trying to put out of her mind for a week now. She

refused to think about any of it. Not the way he'd
been such a comforting source of strength that
day in Mississippi. Not the way he'd gently but
insistently coaxed her out of her shell that night.
Not the way he'd held her and touched her as if
she was precious to him, cracking open the protective shell she'd built around herself, exposing
her, weakening her.

Certainly not the way he'd taken off the minute he'd stripped her of her defenses.

What had happened? The question was too ag-
onizing even to entertain. She probably should
have talked to him when he'd called or read his
e-mail before sending it to cyber-hell. But she
couldn't. She simply couldn't.

Nicki turned to leave the room and ran smack
into one of the dining-room chairs. She gave it a
shove. "Nothing happened," she snapped.

"No fooling?" Toni slid off the table and re-
trieved two of the wallpaper samples from the
corner. "Then this incredibly nasty snit you're in
is just the next level of your natural state, I suppose? Is that it, Slick-Nick?"

"Go jump off the dock, Toni."

Toni held up the wallpaper swatches and studied them a moment. She tossed one at Nicki.

"Here. Use this above the chair rail, and below the chair rail, paint it electric blue."

Catching the square of wallpaper, Nicki sighed. Her cousin was right of course. She'd been a royal pain. But surely she had cause. Then again, maybe she should take her young cousin's favorite advice.

Get over it.

The hot sting of tears surprised her. She squeezed her eyes shut and lowered her head, willing the moment to pass.

Get over it. Of course that was the answer. But how?

Drawing a deep breath, she turned to Toni, who gazed at her with way too much compassion. Swallowing the lump in her throat, she looked down at the gold fleur-de-lis wallpaper Toni had tossed at her. "With electric blue?" she said.

Toni grinned. "Yeah. Why not? Sort of fits the family, don't you think?"

Nicki wasn't sure if the sound bubbling out of her was chuckle or sob or a little of both. "Probably."

Toni walked over and gave her a quick hug. "Either that or pick the taupe stripes and the soft brown paint, and we'll pretend we're something we're not. Who knows, we might fool 'em.''

Nicki longed for another hug, a longer hug. But she didn't know how to ask for it. "You're a peach for putting up with me.''

Toni shrugged. "I have emotional reserves I've hardly begun to tap. If I can put up with my mother, I can put up with anything.''

Nicki managed a smile for her cousin's benefit.

"Gotta run, Nick. Got a rehearsal, then an audition. And maybe a date tonight.''

As they walked to the front porch, Toni slung an arm around her shoulder. Nicki savored the moment of closeness. "A date? Anybody important?''

"I'm eighteen, remember? God forbid it should be anybody important. I have men to conquer and rule before I start hanging with anybody important.''

"Eighteen? I keep forgetting.''

Toni trotted down the front steps. "Hang loose.'' She tossed an impish grin over her shoulder. "Oops. Forgot who I was talking to.''

Nicki actually laughed. Toni laughed, too, as she swung into the front seat of her Jeep and waved goodbye. Nicki watched the vehicle spit gravel and tried to hang on to the cheerfulness

Toni always left behind. She told herself she should be more like her young cousin. Resilient and spirited and vivacious. She knew what Toni's response to her self-flagellation would be. *Cut yourself some slack.*

As the sound of Toni's vehicle faded, another engine roar grew closer. Nicki paused, kept her eyes on the drive. In another moment a familiar sports car rounded the curve and braked at the end of the drive.

A spasm of anguish gripped her. Scott.

She hardened her expression, crossed her arms and prepared to ward off his assault. She would not allow him even a glimpse of her wounds. Furthermore, she would not allow him to invade her home, her privacy, her haven. Never again.

She waited for him to get out of the car, then watched as he approached. He looked wary but determined. Well, so was she. She could match anyone for wary and determined. Even a Lyon could not march in here and turn her life upside down a third time without having one helluva fight on his hands.

He looked thinner, she noticed as he drew closer, his face pinched.

She coached herself to remain cool.

He came onto the porch before he paused and

acknowledged her. Up this close, she saw something in his eyes she might have called remorse had she been willing to grant him that much humanity.

"I need to talk to your grandmother," he said.

Not a word for her. Not a hint of apology. If she'd had long fingernails, she would have scratched his eyes out. "She's not available."

"The same way you weren't available every time I called?" He brushed past her.

She sprang back from the contact as if burned. "Leave her alone!"

Hand on the front door, he turned and looked at her. A retort seemed to tremble on his lips. But he merely stalked into the house without responding. Stunned at his audacity, she followed him, her anger quickly rising to a boil. She followed him into the family room, where Maman Riva sat staring into the ashes in the fireplace.

"Uh-oh! Uh-oh!" That was Perdu.

Even the cats scattered, as if aware that some uncontrollable force had entered the room. Only Milo remained, and he ambled up to Scott, tail wagging.

"You return," Riva said without looking up.

"I have news," Scott said.

Nicki had the strangest feeling that the two of

them were reading from some script that no one had bothered to pass on to her. "Now, listen—"

"The police will probably be out here sometime today," Scott continued.

A cold hard terror crept through Nicki. "What?"

Riva did not seem taken aback by the news. She nodded. Perdu repeated his previous commentary on the situation.

The front door slammed. Nicki jumped. Beau burst into the room, a big smile on his friendly face. "You find your way back, *mon ami.*" He slapped Scott on the back. "We're thinking you lost your way. And this woman here, she—"

"Shut up, Beau!" Nicki said.

Beau began to laugh, then seemed to notice the tension on the three other faces in the room. He ended the laughter abruptly. "What is it?"

Scott stepped toward the fireplace to face Riva. He looked at the old woman when he spoke. "They know you knew Aunt Margaret. They know you worked for Lyon Broadcasting."

Nicki looked at her grandmother. The old woman nodded, one slight dip of her snowy-white head.

Nicki felt ill. The news didn't even surprise her. Hadn't she suspected some connection all along, something secretive going on with her grandmother and the Lyon family? Her heart raced. The police were coming. There was more to know. More knots to unravel in the Bechet family.

"I saw the scrapbook," Scott said, his voice low and tortured. "I had to tell them."

Beau stepped forward and put a hand on Riva's slumped shoulder. "What the hell are you talking about, Lyon?"

Riva waved her grandson to silence, then gestured to the cluttered table beside her chair. Nicki saw it, a large brown album of some kind, frayed at the edges, with scraps of yellowed paper poking out from its edges. She backed away. Beau reached for the album and opened it.

"Maman, what is this about?"

Nicki tried to keep her eyes off the book, but she couldn't. She saw that the first page held a newspaper clipping, a very old newspaper clipping, with the name Lyon in the headline. Her stomach began to twist and turn. She put her hand on her forehead. "Beau, don't—"

All four of them seemed to hear gravel crunching in the driveway at the same time. Beau marched to the window. He turned back to the room with a grim expression. "New Orleans police."

"Maman—"

"Mrs. Bechet, I—"

"Out!" Riva lurched up from her chair, waving her arms at the three young people. Perdu squawked. "All of you, out!"

Beau and Nicki started to protest.

"Show them in and leave us be."

The old woman thrust out her chin and gripped the back of her chair.

"But Maman," Nicki said softly, "you don't have to do this. The Lyons don't run the universe. I'm an attorney, let me—"

"Enough!" The old woman's voice was stronger than Nicki had heard it in years. The doorbell rang. "Show them in."

SCOTT SAT ON A CHAIR on the front porch to wait. Beau sat across from him, scowling. Nicki came out and stood over them, arms tightly crossed, face impassive. Scott suspected she was ready to erupt.

"You've done all the damage you can do," she said sharply. "We would like you to leave now."

He looked at her. On his way out here, he had

tried to put her out of his mind. Had tried to focus solely on his mission—warning Riva. Warning Nicki. It was the least he could do, after opening them up to scrutiny and publicity and God knows what kind of problems.

Yes, he'd tried to put Nicki out of his mind, but he'd failed. All the way down here, his mind had been full of her. He had anticipated the cold fury in her blue eyes masking the stark fear in her heart. He had pictured in perfect detail the way her fair hair would feather in unconscious disarray around her high forehead, her sharp-boned face, her fair cheeks. He had spent the hour alone in his car with too many memories of her lithe, agile body to keep him company.

And here she was in person. And here he was, overcome by her, bewitched by her. How pale everything he'd ever called love seemed in comparison to what he felt for this woman. Oh, Lord, what a mess.

"Now you know why I left the way I did," he said flatly. "Finding out things here weren't as simple as they seemed, it... I was scared. I know I was wrong. I screwed up. And I can never be sorry enough to make up for that. That's why I kept calling. I wanted to tell you that, to tell you that it wasn't about us. About you. But—''

He stopped. He'd said enough. Because in truth there wasn't anything more he could do to make up for hurting her. Now she had to open her heart enough to understand he hadn't wanted to hurt her.

Nicki crossed to the porch rail and gave a wicker basket of fern a mighty heave over the edge. She wheeled to face him. "I should have shot you dead the day you walked onto the property!"

"This we could do now, Nick-o," Beau said calmly. "Save them police another trip out. Get you charged and jailed quick-like."

Nicki ignored Beau. "Is that what brought you out here the first time?" she asked Scott, the words as sharp and seething as the expression on her face. "To snoop around?"

"Your grandmother brought me out here the first time," Scott said.

Nicki pursed her lips. When she spoke again, her voice quavered with the attempt to control it. "You honestly believe an eighty-four-year-old woman is involved in some kind of plot against your family?"

"I honestly believe there's something going on here I don't understand."

He held her gaze, tried to will his thoughts into her. *I love you and I was wrong. I hurt you because of my own fears. I understand why you hurt and I understand why you don't trust me.*

He also wanted to tell her he would make it up to her.

But he couldn't tell her that, because he wasn't sure it was possible. He might not be able to make it up to her. He could only love her, and that might never be enough.

He prayed that wouldn't be the case.

"Let it go, Nicki," Beau said. "Is all just a big misunderstanding. The policemen, they will straighten it out. You'll see."

Nicki turned her glare on her cousin. Then she stomped down the front steps and disappeared around the corner of the house.

Scott forced himself not to follow her.

Beau chuckled and shook his head. "Hoo-whee! One minute that woman is ice. Next minute she's a firecracker. You sure you want something to do with that, Scotty?"

Scott didn't reply. He didn't feel entitled to Beau Bechet's goodwill. But Beau didn't seem to mind the slight. He started to rock and whistle and wait. Scott made himself wait, as well.

NICKI SAT ON THE GROUND, back pressed to the side of the house, fingers clutching and releasing the cool damp soil. She hated Scott Lyon. She hated his arrogant, perfect family. She hated what they were putting her grandmother through. And she feared the publicity that might follow, publicity that could rob her of this safe haven, rob her of Cachette en Bayou.

She wanted to scream, release her outrage into the heavy air. Instead, she yanked a clump of weeds out of the ground and flung it with all her strength. She still wanted to scream.

How could all this be happening? How could so many things be going wrong all at once? And how could she have so many impossible-to-resolve feelings about one man, wanting him even while she hated him?

The creak of the front door sounded. She leapt to her feet and rounded the side of the house to see the uniformed officers descending the front stairs. She confronted them on the way to their vehicle.

''What did she tell you?'' Nicki demanded.

The tall one looked at the taller one, then back

at Nicki. "Maybe you need to ask Mrs. Bechet that question, miss."

Nicki doubted it would help her case to tell them Maman Riva wasn't likely to tell her granddaughter a thing. "I don't want to upset her any more than you already have. But I have a right to know. I'm an attorney."

"Do you represent Mrs. Bechet?"

Nicki hesitated. "Yes."

"Well, miss, you might want to take that up with Mrs. Bechet, since she told us she didn't want an attorney present."

An alarm went off in Nicki's head. Did that mean they'd Mirandized her? Surely not. "You're charging her with something?"

"No."

"You mean, not yet?" she asked.

He slipped his cap on and moved to one side. "If you'll excuse us, miss, it's a long drive back to the city."

They had no intention of telling her anything, and badgering them would only make them hostile. They walked around her, and she found herself staring at the house. At Scott.

He was standing on the porch, his gaze trained on her. She wished she could trust the look of concern in his eyes. She wished she could look at him without feeling the heat between them. She wished this longing for what she'd tasted with him would go away and leave her alone.

She'd been fine before he showed up, despite what everybody else in the family thought. Damn him for making her think that maybe Toni and Maman and Beau were right, that things in her life weren't fine just the way they were.

She approached the house, planning to stalk past him. He closed a hand around her upper arm and stopped her.

"I'm sorry," he said. "About all of it."

She wanted to wrangle with him until he wore her down with his soft voice and his intense eyes, until she once again believed the myth that life could be a place of joy and intimacy. "I'm sure you are. Now if you'll excuse me, I want to make sure my grandmother is all right."

His hand dropped away from her arm. It was a struggle to make herself walk away from him. She was a fool to feel the way she felt about him. She knew that.

She went into the house and shut the door behind her decisively.

CHAPTER ELEVEN

THE INFORMATION on her computer screen gave Nicki the first rush of interest and excitement she'd felt in days. She stared at the words, hands shaking as they hovered over the keyboard.

Debra Brackett Minor had attended nursing school at a community college in Tallahassee, Florida.

Nicki touched the words on her screen with her fingertips, as if she could make an emotional connection that way. Her mother had wanted to be a nurse. The woman who gave birth to her had decided to enter a healing profession when she was thirty-five years old. Almost the same age Nicki was now.

She brought her fingertips to her lips and continued to stare at the screen. She *did* feel something as she gained this glimpse into the life of the first person who had walked away from her. She wanted to believe that Debra Brackett Minor had taken charge of her life.

But Debra, she learned, had dropped out before finishing. And she had never bothered to look up her daughter, who would have been so easy to find.

Nicki stood, stretching her back and rubbing her hands together. Damned old house was chilly despite the revamped heating system. She glanced at the clock and realized she'd been hunched over the computer for two hours. This morning's search had been the first thing to capture her attention in the two days since the police had been here.

Since Scott had been here.

Fighting her weariness, Nicki headed for the kitchen for a cup of hot tea. Maybe she would explore some additional records now that she knew her mother had shown an interest in nursing. She could have finished her schooling elsewhere. She could be working in a hospital. Who knows, maybe she'd decided to become a doctor, instead of a nurse.

Riva was chopping onion. She chopped slowly, methodically. Perdu offered helpful tips from his perch on her shoulder. Riva did not respond to the cockatiel's conversation. She had not joined in many conversations since her interview with the New Orleans police officers.

Nicki filled the copper kettle with water and set it on a burner. Turning the burner on, she propped one hip against the stove and studied her grandmother. The old woman worried her. She was wearing beige today. Nicki had never seen her grandmother in beige. If asked, she would have sworn Maman Riva did not own a garment in such a drab, uninspiring color. Riva wore purple, red, gold, turquoise. Not beige.

"I'll cook tonight," Nicki said. She pulled a cup and saucer from the dish drainer, a teabag from a small container. "You should rest."

"Makes me no mind," Riva said, continuing to chop.

"I'll do *étouffée*. T-John's recipe."

"Leave me be. I can still cook."

Her voice sounded as lifeless as she looked. Panic seeped into Nicki's heart. What if her grandmother was dying? She set her cup on the counter and moved closer to Riva. She smelled gardenia talcum powder and wintergreen breath mints. She smiled. How would the world keep revolving without gardenia talc and wintergreen mints?

"Talk to me," she said softly. The kettle whistled.

"Talk? Me, I have work. No time for talk."

Again, the listless way Riva spoke alarmed Nicki. She wanted to touch her grandmother, to reassure herself with the woman's warmth. She settled, instead, for pouring steaming water over the teabag in an old china cup. She cupped her fingers around it for warmth and held it close to her face, inhaling the fragrant steam.

"Tell me about the Lyons," she said.

"Nothing to tell."

"Is that what you told the police?"

Riva gave the mound of onions a vicious whack. "You make love with that Scott?"

"Maman—"

"See. Nobody likes a Nosy Nellie."

"But I'm worried about you. You're moping around here like—"

"Like my granddaughter mopes around. You stay out of my business, I stay out of yours. Deal?"

Nicki stiffened and took a sip of her tea before she replied. "You made it my business when you dragged him into my life."

"I'm old. When you're old, you can be a Nosy Nellie, too. My permission, you have it this instant. Now, get out of my kitchen." She waved the chopping knife toward the door.

Nicki sighed. "Okay. You win."

Riva nodded. "Good. I win."

Impulsively, Nicki set down her teacup long enough to touch the back of her grandmother's hand. "I love you, Maman. I— Good gracious, your hands are like ice. Where's your shawl?"

Riva shook her head. "Upstairs somewhere. I don't know."

"I'll get it for you. You're freezing."

Riva was grumbling as Nicki exited the kitchen and went in search of the shawl she rarely saw her grandmother without. Even with all the renovations, the big high-ceilinged house was like a barn, cool and damp. She supposed she would have to insulate the blasted place on top of everything else.

FEAR DID NOT CROP UP easily when you were eighty-four, Riva thought. There wasn't much in life that threatened you at that age.

You could die, but surely what came after could be no more difficult than what you'd already experienced.

You could grow sicker or more infirm.

Disgrace could befall you; Riva figured that was overdue in her case, anyway.

None of those things worried her.

She put the chopping knife down on the

counter, wiped her hands on a towel and crossed to the window. She stared out over the land, the sheltering trees, which brought shadows as the price they exacted for their protective shade.

There was always a price. Riva had learned that long ago.

Her fondest hope had always been that the only price paid would be hers. She knew now that it wasn't so. Never had been so.

She was weak with fear that it was all catching up with her. She had brought it on more than fifty years ago, when she had first concocted a scheme to sidestep the consequences of her wicked ways. She had paid for her actions every day of her life, and that was as it should be. At least her innocent child hadn't had to suffer every day for his mother's sins.

Her son had been both blessed and a blessing for those who had taken him into their heart and home.

And now what had she done but betray her part of the bargain? She had violated her word to the woman she admired most in the world, by bringing their families together and jeopardizing the secret.

It would all come to light now and it would be her fault.

. A part of her almost hoped Margaret Lyon was dead so she would never have to know that Riva had betrayed her. But even if Margaret never knew, others would. The truth was bound to come out and people would be hurt, including her precious Nicki.

Including the son she had denied.

NICKI DIDN'T FIND the shawl in the parlor, so she climbed the stairs to Riva's room. The door was closed, as it rarely was. She let herself in and found the room in chaos. The discovery momentarily stalled her in her tracks. Maman Riva was never tidy, but this was chaos. The ancient eight-foot-high chiffonier—built from local cypress a century earlier by Riva's father—gaped open, its stash of boxes scattered on the floor.

Nicki shook her head. What was going on with her grandmother these days? She leaned over to scoop up one of the boxes. Photos and papers and bundles of envelopes were strewn every-where, almost as if Riva had decided to review her life—

The thought stopped Nicki cold.

Wasn't that what people did as they prepared to die?

Fighting the impulse to begin a frantic snoop

through the debris of Maman Riva's eighty-four years, Nicki wrapped her arms around her waist and tried to tell herself that a certain amount of looking back was normal at her grandmother's age. Why, here she was with no one else around her who remembered the same things she remembered, so who wouldn't want to indulge in a little reminiscing from time to time?

The rationalization wouldn't fly.

Nicki glanced around the room. She spotted the purple shawl Riva wore on all but the most sweltering summer days. It was draped over the back of the chair at the cluttered desk beside the window. Reminding herself that her grandmother was downstairs shivering, Nicki crossed to the chair to retrieve the shawl.

She did not intend to look at whatever was spread out on the desk.

What caught her eye was the purple silk ribbon. Maman Riva had a thing for purple. Whatever she had tied in purple silk ribbon—it appeared to be a stack of correspondence of some sort—must be important. Nicki hesitated.

The envelopes and half-folded papers were elegant cream-colored parchment, distinguished by a single gold-embossed letter. The letter *L*.

Nicki's breath caught.

She put her hand on the shawl, told herself to keep moving. But if the papers had been guarded by the meanest gator in the swamp, she would have been unable to stop herself from leaning closer.

The date was December 4, 1961, written in a very economical script across the top.

"My dearest Riva," it began.

Nicki gasped. A love letter? Nicki's mouth went dry. She picked up the letter. She knew it was wrong, but she had to know.

"I think of you today, as always. I know things have been rocky for your family. Please accept the enclosed as a token of gratitude for your generosity and your silence, which keeps my family together."

It was signed Margaret.

Nicki dropped the letter. She felt nauseated with fear. It wasn't a love letter at all. Then what? She quickly riffled through the papers and saw that the rest of the small stack also carried the gold-embossed letter.

Her grandmother knew Margaret Lyon. They had corresponded through the years.

No, it was more than that. *A token of gratitude for your…silence.* To all appearances, Maman Riva had been blackmailing Margaret Lyon.

CHAPTER TWELVE

"WHEN ARE YOU GOING BACK to work?"

It was the question everyone wanted an answer to, and Scott wasn't happy to hear it again from his next-door neighbor. In the two days since he'd gone out to Bayou Sans Fin, he'd been able to think of little else but how much pain he'd caused Nicki. He lifted the empty pizza box off the coffee table and headed to the kitchen with it.

"Not that we don't love volunteers." Donnie followed him and rummaged in the refrigerator for another can of beer. He came up empty. "Your life is falling apart, man. No job, no woman, no beer."

"I'm simplifying," Scott said, crushing the box and shoving it into the trash can on top of the one from the night before.

Donnie grunted. "I know you're not going to start living off the relatives at this late date. So what's the plan?"

"Did I invite you over to stand in for my mother?"

"I invited myself. And I should've brought beer, too."

Scott responded to his friend's easy grin with a forced smile. "Come on. Halftime's almost over."

Donnie sprawled in one recliner, Scott in the other. He pointed the remote at the TV and turned it up, hoping to discourage any conversation other than the occasional mild profanity directed at a clumsy play. Donnie was a good guy; perhaps too good. That was the problem. He'd lived in the town house next door to Scott for three years now, and despite his ribbing about the beer, he wasn't known for the excesses some single men indulged in. Donnie was a minister whose wife had walked out, leaving him adrift and unsure of his place in his chosen profession. Ever since, he'd been serving as volunteer co-ordinator for a number of service agencies in the city. Scott had been one of his regular volunteers for years; in the past week Scott had worked in the community almost as many hours a day as Donnie.

Scott was glad for the company tonight. Glad for anything that kept his mind off Nicki.

He couldn't think when he'd mucked up the waters with a woman worse. He'd known from the very beginning that she was fragile. Since before the beginning, actually, from the moment he'd pointed a camera at her a few years ago and seen the anguish in her eyes. She'd played it tough and gotten away with it, thanks in part to that imposing black robe she wore in those days. But Scott had known what he was seeing, and she had merely confirmed it when she took off and ran.

She was still playing it tough, with her overalls and her shotgun and that steely glint in her eyes.

But the truth was, she was as fragile as ever. And he'd managed to get past the black robe and the shotgun and the steely glint.

And what had he done? Betrayed her. Won two ounces of trust from her and repaid it by walking out the moment her defenses were down. By charging in with an ugly accusation and the police and the promise of more of the same kind of ugly publicity that had sent her running before.

"Must be weighing pretty heavy on your mind."

Donnie's voice startled him. "Huh?"

"Whatever you're thinking about. You just missed the go-ahead touchdown."

"Oh."

"I know it's not a very guy kind of thing, but I am a good listener."

Unloading wasn't a bad idea. But Scott hadn't had enough beer for that. "Sure. Thanks, Don."

"If you're not going to tell me what's eating you, at least watch the game. I hate watching alone, okay?"

Scott could do that; he could force himself to put Nicki out of his mind and concentrate on football for a few hours. Surely. "You got it."

They were roaring in outrage over a clear-cut case of blind referees and a blatant holding penalty when the doorbell rang twenty minutes later.

Nobody came to see Scott at this hour of the night, unless it was one of his rotten-tempered brothers. He considered ignoring the bell. He glanced at Donnie, saw the speculative gaze his friend directed at him.

"Okay, okay."

Psyching himself for a face-to-face with Alain or Raymond, Scott headed for the door.

NICKI CONSIDERED ringing the bell again. She could hear the sounds of the TV on the other side of the door, so he had to be home. But a part of her would have been glad for the opportunity to turn around and return to her car. She could say she'd given it her best shot.

But she owed him an apology.

She rubbed her temple, where her head had throbbed all day, ever since she'd discovered her grandmother's letters. Maybe it was keeping the secret that was giving her the headache. She should have thrown out all the incriminating stuff, anything Riva had in her possession that would link her to the Lyons. What if the police came back with a search warrant?

Oh, yes, her head was throbbing in earnest now.

If only she could have had it out with Maman Riva, demanded the truth and held her ground no matter how stubborn the old woman became. She might have, too, if her grandmother hadn't looked so beaten down these past few days. If she couldn't speak with Maman, who else was left that she could tell? One of her life-is-a-party cousins?

The only person she could imagine discussing this with was Scott, and that, of course, was impossible.

But she did owe Scott an apology for judging him, for directing her anger at him. He was simply concerned about a family member. She had to clear the air, if only to clear her conscience.

Maybe if she could do that much, she wouldn't have to reveal the rest of what she now knew. Maybe then she could figure out what to do next. Because she, too, was concerned about a family member and would do whatever it took to safeguard her.

She raised her hand to ring the bell one more time when the door swung open.

"Scott."

"Nicki."

She shivered. He might as well have touched her, the sound of his voice caressing her name was so intimate. She was in danger of losing herself in his eyes, in his voice, in his arms.

"Well, we've established you know each other," came another voice from behind Scott. "Are you going to invite her in?"

"Oh—"

"Oh—"

Scott moved a step to allow her to enter; she backed away a step.

"You have company."

"No, I—"

"I'll—I should have called. I'll—"

"No, it's fine. Please, I—"

A tall lean man with a speculative smile appeared in the doorway. "Actually, I was just leaving. He's out of beer and he's let the other team go ahead three touchdowns."

Nicki felt heat coloring her cheeks. "No, I—"

"See you around, Scott. And nice to meet you, Nicki."

Then the man with the friendly face was gone, leaving her alone in the doorway with a man whose face looked as confused and uncertain as she herself felt.

"Come in," he said.

She'd done the wrong thing, coming here. She knew that now. She didn't want to be in his home, alone with him. Did she?

She walked in. The door closed behind her with an ominous finality. She tried to look around the room, to concentrate on the details of his home. But she was aware of only one thing, the man himself—his closeness, the heat and power of his presence. He wore sweatpants and a T-shirt molded to his chest. She remembered that chest. She knew how it felt against her cheek, her lips, her breasts.

No, this was not the right direction for her thoughts.

She moved farther into the room, away from him.

He followed.

"Have a seat."

There were two recliners. That looked safe enough, as long as she didn't recline. She sat. He sat, pointed the clicker at the TV. The sound disappeared. The pumped-up men on the field continued lunging at one another.

She swallowed hard and made herself look at him.

Looking at him almost undid her.

Scott Lyon wasn't like other men Nicki knew. In her experience, men came in two packages—ultra-slick or ultra-macho. Her father, Steve Walthan and several of her cousins were the first kind—good looking, charming and completely self-absorbed. Most of the other men she knew out here at Bayou Sans Fin were the second type—real he-men who were more bluster than finesse.

But Scott was neither. His good looks were quiet, easy to overlook at first. Even the way he carried himself demanded no attention. There was no arrogance in him, no bluster. And the way he'd made love with her had been quiet, tender. And that had been far more meaningful than the

lovemaking she'd experienced in the past, text-
book lovemaking designed to elicit a response,
not convey an emotion. She knew the difference
now.

"I'm glad you came," he said, disarming her
all over again.

She nodded, but had trouble looking him in the
eye. She had to get this over with quickly, before
she did something foolish. "I came to say I'm
sorry. Sorry I was so angry."

"I understand why you were angry."

He would. "I feel protective. Of my grandmother."

"And I walked out on you."

He was right of course. But she didn't have to
admit that out loud. She could hold on to that
much dignity. She shook her head. "No, I can
see why you did. You were worried about your
aunt."

He reached across the end table that separated
their chairs and touched her hand, brushed the
back of it really, with his fingertips. "I was
wrong, doing it that way. It wasn't what I wanted
to do. I got frightened."

She looked at him, startled both by the touch
and the admission. His eyes were so gray, like a
breath of fog across the bayou. "You?"

"We're all frightened sometimes, Nicki."

He made it so easy for her to feel she could trust him. She longed to tell him everything—not just her fears about what she'd learned about her grandmother and his aunt, but her fears about herself. Her inadequacy, her shortcomings. He would understand. She knew that. He would comfort her.

And then he would leave her again. Wouldn't he?

"Are we?" She tried to sound like her tough cynical self, but doubted she'd pulled it off.

He nodded.

"What in the world would a Lyon be afraid of?" she asked with a little laugh that didn't come out nearly as nonchalantly as she'd hoped.

"The same things you are. Not fitting in. Not belonging. Being used. Never being loved just for who you are."

She swallowed hard. "You're making that up."

"No, I'm not. I've been living it for thirty-four years. And so have you."

She didn't want him delving into her heart and soul that way, but she didn't seem to know how to stop him. He really did seem to understand.

But she wanted the things he understood not to be true. She wanted to be different. To change.

"Sometimes we have to find people who understand us just the way we are before we can begin to change," Scott said. "Finding someone who understands us, that's the first step."

She shuddered at his apparent ability to read her mind. She reinstated her defenses. "I'm fine the way I am. I don't need to change."

"You shut yourself off to life."

She stood. "I should go."

He stood and grasped her hands before she could step away. "You don't have to live that way anymore."

She thought of the letters and her grandmother and his aunt. And none of it was as compelling at that moment as the touch of his hands on hers and the way his eyes commanded the truth from her. Her need for him was so pure and simple it overrode everything.

"I don't want to," she whispered. "But—"

"Let's show each other how to live," he said.

"I…" She couldn't think. He must be right. He was surely right, because she had never felt as alive as she did now.

She moved into his arms.

A little voice in her head began its shrill warning.

She shushed it by touching her lips to his.

He cupped her head with his hand, a gesture of infinite tenderness. His mouth covered hers, warm and sweet. She slipped her arms around his neck and pressed herself to the solid length of him.

"I won't leave this time," he whispered as he slid a hand beneath her shirt.

She remembered vaguely that there was a reason he might want to leave. But whatever it was mattered much less than this moment.

Unhurriedly she let him help her shed her clothes, helped him do the same. She savored each inch of skin and muscle as it was revealed and accepted his caresses as a gift in return. With each touch, all fear and loneliness seemed to empty out of her and she welcomed Scott into the spaces left there.

LYING WITH NICKI in his arms the next morning was disconcerting.

Scott couldn't help but remember the last time they'd made love, watching her sleep but unable to sleep himself, and what had happened after.

He frowned. Last night it had all seemed so simple.

She stirred and looked up at him. He saw the wariness that had returned to her eyes. She didn't move away, but he felt the difference in her body. She was no longer relaxed, no longer lulled by their lovemaking.

She inched the sheet a little higher, covered her breasts, a signal to him that it was time to confront their problems head-on.

"What made you come here?" he asked.

She stared at the ceiling. "I told you. I wanted to say I was sorry."

"What changed your mind?"

She shifted away from him, tucked the sheet further around her naked body.

"You know something, don't you?" he persisted.

She flinched; he was sure of it.

"What is it, Nicki? If you tell me, we can work it out together. Whatever it is that's between our families, we can fix it together. I love you, and I think you love me."

She closed her eyes. "I don't know anything that will help us."

Frustrated, he sprang up from the bed and

pulled on a pair of sweatpants. "Uncovering all the secrets—that's what will help us."

She stood, too, dragging the sheet with her. "Leave it alone, Scott."

"I can't leave it alone. My aunt's life may be at stake." He saw the torture of indecision in her eyes. "Our life together is at stake."

"Don't." Her eyes filled with tears.

"We can survive the truth, Nicki. But no love can survive the lies."

Tears spilled onto her cheeks, but she said, "I'd like to get dressed now."

He wanted to tell her he loved her again. And again and again until she couldn't close her heart to it. Until she had to tell him what was in her heart. He wanted to wear her down until she was swamped by the feelings she'd denied for so long that she no longer believed they existed. He knew better. But he was beginning to doubt he had it in him to convince her.

He left the room.

NICKI DRESSED.

What if he was right? What if the two of them together could overcome this hidden evil between their families?

First you'll have to believe in the kind of love he's talking about.

She hid in the bathroom, unable to prepare herself to face him. She splashed her face with water, waited for every sign of tears to vanish. She waited for the resolve that had always seen her through everything.

It was almost daylight when she finally came out.

The town house was empty. She found a note tacked to the front door:

"Nicki," it began, "I've gone to get breakfast. Please wait. We can work this out together. I know we can. I love you and I know you love me. I felt it last night. That counts for something. You know it does—Scott"

She crushed the note in her fist and stood for a moment, paralyzed by uncertainty. She wanted to believe him. But she also knew the price she would pay, the price her family would pay. Scandal and heartbreak, perhaps worse.

She'd paid that price once before.

She grabbed her purse and walked out, hoping he wouldn't return before she made it to her car.

HE CAME HOME with hot fluffy biscuits and a selection of eggs and bacon and juice from his fa-

vorite neighborhood diner. He didn't see her car
when he pulled into his parking space.

"No," he muttered, leaving the bags of food
on the seat of the car and dashing to his front
door. "No, no, no."

She was gone. All she'd left behind was her
scent—on the sheets, on the towel, in the air.

That, and the aching emptiness inside him.

He couldn't stay here alone. He ate a bit of
the breakfast, threw the remainder in the trash,
then set out, fighting the urge to go after her. He
played a game of pool at a dive near the river.
He drove by the volunteer center but changed his
mind, anticipating Donnie's questions. He ate
lunch alone and barely choked down a third of a
muffuletta. He found himself in his car again and
knew he had to distract himself before he ended
up at Cachette en Bayou.

He went to WDIX-TV. Maybe he could round
up a few of his buddies for a little barhopping
tonight. Maybe he'd find out if Crystal had a gig
somewhere and he could go see a performance.
Maybe he'd pick a fight with Raymond.

It turned out his frame of mind was best suited
to this last idea.

He made small talk with his buddies on the
camera crew. He tried a little flirting with Tif-

fany, the newsroom clerk. She was thrilled—he was not. He discovered that his recovering work-aholic cousin Crystal had already left for the day, on her way to an open house at her adopted son's school.

So he barged into Raymond's office.

His brother wasn't there, either. But there were signs that Raymond would be back soon. The computer was up and running. The mug of coffee sitting beside the mouse pad still steamed. Scott decided to wait.

He prowled the room, spoiling for a fight. He plucked a ratings book off the shelf, flipped through it to see how the station stacked up against the competition. He couldn't concentrate on the columns of numbers. It was senseless, anyway. In the grand scheme of things, who gave a damn whether WDIX-TV evening news came out two percentage points ahead of the other stations in town? Stacked against family and love and loyalty, how important were ratings and market share?

As he shoved the book back onto the shelf, he spotted a glossy folder that had apparently slipped behind the other books. He plucked it out and tossed it onto Raymond's desk. When he did, the contents spilled out.

The folder was stuffed with brochures on nursing homes.

Scott frowned. Were Raymond and Alain plotting to put their father in a nursing home? Sure, the old man dithered a little these days and didn't always make sense. But they had the money to look after him without sticking him in a nursing home. Scott's mood grew into anger. They had no right to consider this without talking to him about it. This was a family decision and no one in the family had ever once mentioned a nursing home.

Scott's heart sped up.

Except once.

A few months ago he'd overheard Raymond say to Alain, *The old battle-ax ought to be locked up. She's too old to be sticking her nose in things here. Lock her up in an old folks' home, where she can't do any more harm. That's what we ought to do.*

No, that was too farfetched even for Raymond. This little discovery had nothing to do with Aunt Margaret's disappearance.

But Scott no longer wanted to wait for his brother. Taking the folder with him, he left WDIX-TV and went back to his house. He stewed for hours, staring blankly at the sports network on the TV. Finally he picked up the telephone and dialed Cachette en Bayou.

Nicki answered. Her voice took his breath away. He reminded himself that he had one reason and one reason only for calling.

"If Aunt Margaret was in a nursing home, could we find her?"

"Well, of course. Eventually."

"Even if she was registered under some other name?"

"What's this about, Scott?"

He repeated his question. "Could we find her?"

"Possibly."

She sounded cold and stiff, and it hurt. Hurt like hell.

"Will you...will you help me?"

She hesitated. "Yes."

"Good. I'll be right out."

"No! No, that's not a good idea. Just...give me a little information first. I'll get on the computer tonight."

If only he could see her, be with her. Touch her. How could she mistrust him when she could look into his eyes and see how much he loved her? But if she wouldn't even see him, what chance did he have? He sighed. "Okay. What do you need?"

She asked some questions. He answered as best he could, even suggesting the name of some of the nursing homes in Raymond's folder, without saying where he'd gotten the names. She was all business. So was he. It was best that way. Then she hung up.

Dammit, but he wanted to cry. His whole blasted world was falling apart around him.

CHAPTER THIRTEEN

SCOTT SURVEYED the standing-room-only courtroom. It was full of Lyons—brothers, father, cousins, in-laws.

"Huge irony, wouldn't you say?" That was Crystal, perching beside Scott on the tiny wedge of back row that remained.

"How's that?" he whispered back.

"When was the last time you saw the entire family together like this?"

He glanced at his cousin and saw in her face a jumble of emotions that matched his own. He nodded at her assessment. Apparently what it took to bring the family together was a courtroom hearing on his brothers' injunction against André's inheritance.

Scott had purposely planted himself in the back of the crowded courtroom, as far away from all the Lyons as he could get, shamed and angered by the spectacle of his family's squabble. Of course, the city's news media was out in force, including a crew from WDIX-TV, because André had too much integrity to try sweeping the situation under the rug. After today's preliminary hearing, the story wouldn't be out of the news until the court battle was resolved.

"I see you're not with your brothers," Crystal whispered as everyone rose for the judge's entrance.

"And you're not with André."

Crystal shrugged. "Listen, all I can think of is how fast this bunch would scatter if Aunt Margaret came walking in right this minute. I just want it over."

Scott nodded, shifting to make more room for his cousin. They listened intently to the arguments, but Scott also kept one eye on various members of the family. He hoped no one would notice him—not his brothers, his father, his cousins. The accusations from his brothers made him want to bolt from the courtroom more than once—there were references to alleged evidence that André was not a Lyon, allegations of Margaret Lyon's intent to defraud the family and more.

"Anyone who can't see that André is the spitting image of Uncle Paul needs an eye exam," Crystal whispered in his ear at one point.

Scott gave a curt nod to indicate his agree-
ment. ''Not to mention the fact that anyone who
believes Aunt Margaret would defraud the family
is clearly a brick or two shy of a load.''

Crystal gave him a grateful smile; her eyes had
misted over. He squeezed her arm; he knew how
close she'd been to Aunt Margaret. It struck him
at that moment how remarkable Aunt Margaret
was, that she could be so intimately involved
with so many in her family. She had truckloads
of compassion and she never hesitated to spread
it around.

Thank goodness she was being spared this
spectacle.

As lunchtime neared, Scott's sense of outrage
grew. And by the time the judge ruled that there
was probable cause for Alain's claim, Scott was
ready to take a whack at something or someone.
He spotted Alain and Raymond up front, smugly
clapping each other on the back.

''I'm taking off,'' he said to Crystal as the
crowd began to move out of the courtroom, ''before I do something they'll have to drag me into
court for.''

His cousin gave him a hug, and he shouldered
his way toward the door.

He saw her at the door, two steps ahead of

him. Nicki. He hadn't seen her since the morning at his place, although they'd spoken by phone a few times. Staying in touch and getting updates were good excuses for hearing her voice and for hanging on to the hope that something would change.

Today she wore dark pants and a black jacket that looked as if it might have been left over from one of her suits from the old days. She looked unsure of herself; she glanced around furtively, as if afraid someone would recognize her.

He began directing his pent-up anger and frustration toward her—a safer target.

They reached the door at the same instant. Looking guilty, she glanced away and pushed her way out of the crowd. He kept his eyes on her until they both broke free of the mob. He caught up with her at a back exit, away from the spectators and media.

"I suppose you enjoyed watching the high-and-mighty Lyons airing dirty linen," he said bitterly.

She stopped and turned to face him. "I thought I might. But I was wrong."

He felt his anger slipping away. Dammit, why did he always go soft inside around this woman? "Were you?"

There was a raw honesty in her face that made his query unnecessary.

She pursed her lips and wrapped her arms protectively around her middle. "Looking at your family…it was like looking at myself. They seemed so distraught and shell-shocked and… Your cousin André, when they talked about him not even being a Lyon, he seemed to collapse inward."

As she spoke, Scott's anger vanished completely. Nicki wasn't responsible for this morning's scene. And he had no right to take it out on her. He nodded. "André's a strong man, but…"

Nicki drew a deep breath. "I always used to think if you couldn't hold up, it meant you weren't strong enough."

"Maybe it just means you're human."

She smiled wryly. "Now there's a grim possibility."

"It was meant to be some consolation."

"You obviously don't know how hard it is to be human."

He took another step in her direction. "Why don't you tell me?"

She studied him. Her hands began to relax their grip on her arms. Her voice dropped to a whisper. ''You know what happens when you're human?''

He waited.

''You get hurt.''

She looked down. Her hair swung down to hide her face. He reached up and held it back with one finger. ''You know what happens when you try not to be human?''

She shook her head.

''You get hurt.''

She smiled crookedly. ''So either way, we're in big trouble.''

''Pretty much. The advantage of being human is that at least you get the good stuff that goes along with being human.''

''The good stuff?''

''Sure.'' He smiled at her. ''Friends who love you. Family who stands by you. Babies. Puppies. Kisses and hugs and cold nights under the covers with someone warm.''

He saw the hunger in her eyes. ''But all those things can disappear,'' she said.

''But at least you experienced them. Which is better than denying yourself the pleasure of having them.''

''Is it?''

He took her hand and slipped it into the crook

of his arm. He liked the feel of it there; he liked even better that she didn't pull away. "Yes. Trust me."

She didn't answer, but she started down the stairs and across the parking lot with him. "Where are we going?"

"To the Quarter, to this little hole-in-the-wall take-out joint I know where I'm going to feed you the best crawfish fritters you've ever tasted."

Her gait slowed. "To the Quarter? I don't know. I don't usually go to the French Quarter."

He thought she must be joking. "Everybody goes to the Quarter."

"Not me."

She wasn't joking. He turned to face her, threading his fingers through hers as their arms unlinked. "Why not?"

She looked at him as if she wanted to answer, but the words were beyond her.

"There's nothing there to haunt you."

"Yes, there is."

The lost-child sound of her voice stirred a certain protectiveness in Scott. "Then it's time we chased off anything that's haunting you," he said softly.

"Scott...you don't understand."

"You can tell me."

"No, I... That wouldn't be..."

"Okay. Let's just eat fritters. Maybe have a cold beer. See what happens."

She eased her fingers away from his and shoved them deep into the pockets of her jacket. He could see the wheels spinning in her mind. He wanted desperately to draw her back to him, but he knew that there was too fine a line between bringing her close and scaring her off.

"I'm afraid," she said at last, so softly the traffic from the street almost covered it.

Her admission gave him hope. "Of what?"

"That I'll... It's just that..."

He touched her cheek; she leaned into the touch almost imperceptibly, then stiffened.

"Tell me, Nicki."

She sighed, a burdened quavering breath. "I grew up there. I worked the streets when I was a child." Her face contorted with effort. "Singing. Dancing. I... You..."

It almost did him in not to be able to take her in his arms. "I know that."

"I never go back there."

"Come with me. If you come with me, the place will never have power over you again."

"You don't understand."

"Trust me," he said.

His heart thumped while he waited to see what she would decide this time. She looked bewildered and woebegone.

"Can I? Trust you?"

"Yes."

She searched his face for a sign. She must have seen it, for she took a hesitant step in his direction and slipped her hand into the crook of his arm again.

"Okay. But if I don't like being human, I can always change my mind. Right?"

"You have my word on it."

"CRAWFISH FRITTERS and beer are a wonderful way to ease into being human," Nicki announced forty-five minutes later.

They were walking the streets of the Quarter, which were relatively quiet in early afternoon. Scott held the beer, Nicki held the greasy paper tray of food. She was still nervous about her surroundings, trying to concentrate on the food and the companionship.

"Ah, yes," Scott said. "Deep-fried food. Definitely one of those things that make being human worthwhile. It's bad for you, and that's good. *Laissez les bon temps roulez* and all that jazz."

"You sound like my cousins."

"Thank you."

She laughed, and he joined her.

They finished the food and drink, tossed their trash into a corner barrel and continued to walk. Nicki tried to direct their path toward the outskirts of the Quarter, but Scott kept taking turns that led them closer to Jackson Square. She felt herself tightening up.

"We can leave," he said softly. "But you've come this far."

She nodded. She could leave. It was her choice. Nobody else's.

They passed the building where she'd lived most of her childhood, a centuries-old two-story stucco with elaborate wrought-iron railings and French doors off the upstairs gallery. She glanced up, planned to just keep walking. Instead, her pace slowed: She couldn't take her eyes off the place.

Scott stopped. "What is it?"

She stared up at the old building, painted a spritely shade of mint-green, the wrought iron like a frill of white lace. She felt almost disembodied, as if watching herself from a distance. She wanted to huddle close to Scott, but couldn't manage it. Just being here, in this place, made her feel completely on her own, as if there was nowhere to turn but inward. "It looks different now."

"You remember this building?"

"I lived here."

He covered her hand with his. Comfort seeped through her.

"It was pink then. I hated it. It was so garish. The French doors were falling off their hinges and I had to be careful not to step too close to the railings on the gallery. They were loose, too." She drew a deep breath and looked at him. "Growing up in the Quarter, there were a lot of things a kid had to be careful not to get too close to."

He squeezed the hand he held, but said nothing.

When she'd had her fill of staring, she turned to him, nodded and they began walking again. Down Dauphine and right on Dumaine, right again on Royal, left into Pirate's Alley. She allowed him to lead her to the one place she didn't want to end up. When they stepped clear of the alley, they were in Jackson Square.

Once again, Nicki paused, taking it in.

Jackson Square was a less-than-inspiring patch of green enclosed by a wrought-iron fence. A statue of seventh U.S. president Andrew Jackson, seated on a rearing horse, graced the middle of the small park. St. Louis Cathedral lorded it over the slightly shabby buildings that surrounded the plaza. Formerly buildings of the Spanish government, they now housed apartments, museums, gift shops and restaurants. Horse-drawn carriages collected and deposited passengers on Decatur Street between Jackson Square and the river. And the wrought-iron fence around the plaza was ringed by street performers and tarot readers and palmists and artists.

This had been the face of Jackson Square as far back as Nicki could remember.

This ancient block had been her school, her playground, her church. From lunchtime until bedtime, from the age of four until she hit adolescence, this was the place she called home. Everyone she knew was here, from the free-spirited artists of the sixties and seventies to the aging former hooker who sold flowers. They'd been her friends and her family, her protectors, even. She'd gone home more than once with the flower seller, when her father stepped out for a drink near the end of the day and never returned.

"That was our spot," she said, pointing to a corner nearest an ice-cream shop. "It was shady in the summer. That was important, to find some shade.''

They circled the square slowly, pausing when Nicki dredged up and spit out her memories. It wasn't until they'd made the complete round that she realized what she'd been looking for, and felt the relief of knowing she hadn't seen it.

There were no children performing for tossed coins, no children pandering to the crowd.

Her knees felt wobbly when they finished the circuit. Scott bought her an ice-cream cone and they sat at a little plastic table outside the shop. Now that she'd started, she couldn't stop talking about all she remembered of her childhood. It felt as if she was robbing her past of its power each time she recited another detail and discovered that Scott didn't look at her in disgust.

''You don't despise me,'' she said.

He handed her a napkin. ''Of course not. No one would.''

She closed her eyes. ''But I saw it. In their eyes. When they threw money in his saxophone case.''

''Maybe it wasn't you they despised.''

Her eyes flew open. ''Him?''

He shrugged.

''I never thought of that. Never.''

"You were a child. Children always do that, I think. Whatever is wrong in their lives, they think it's all about them. I did that with my family."

She didn't have to ask what was wrong with the Lyons. The kind of family rift she'd seen in court today didn't brew up in a few days or weeks. She looked at him, and for a fleeting moment the hurt child inside him showed in his eyes. That split second of vulnerability tugged at her heart.

"But you haven't hung on to all that," she said. "You've healed yourself."

"Not entirely. I've just made a little progress. I still have trouble being around it—all the bickering and jealousy."

"At least you've made some progress."

"Maybe today you have, too."

If so, she owed much of it to him. She wanted to tell him that, but when she looked into his eyes, there was so much more to tell him that she couldn't trust herself to begin. If she did, she would end up telling him what she wasn't yet ready to acknowledge.

That she loved him.

And she hadn't yet made that much progress. Admitting her love still seemed too frightening, too much an invitation to disaster.

RIVA HAD BEEN SURPRISED when her grand-daughter decided to go into New Orleans the day the courts took up the Lyon case. But it did offer her the opportunity she needed.

She went into the city herself, but nowhere near the courthouse. Just thinking about what was going on in the courthouse saddened her, for she could imagine how devastated Margaret would have been to know what was happening to her family.

Riva's cabbie friend dropped her off in the Garden District, no questions asked. She found the house she wanted with no trouble; she remembered with clarity the last time she'd loitered outside this very house, waiting for her opportunity.

Her heart had been filled with trepidation that day, too.

It was different now of course. When she'd waylaid a young Margaret Lyon nearly sixty years earlier, the rich residents of the area had been more visible. They'd sometimes ventured into the streets and ridden the streetcar into town. Today, the one she sought pulled up to the back gate in a long, shiny car. Riva's resolve faltered. What now?

She made her way to the gate. It was closing

behind the car when she reached it. He was safely inside the gate and she was safely outside.

An omen?

Her chest hurt. This trip had been difficult. This *decision* had been difficult.

She banged on the gate with her walking stick. A terrible racket.

The car braked. She kept banging.

The car door opened and a man climbed out.

The pain in her chest grew sharp. Stress and fear, that was all. The old quack at home said her heart was strong.

He looked at her, frowning. He was regal in appearance, taller than his father, barely graying at the temples. "Is there some problem?" he asked.

Riva smiled. Some rich men would have cursed a strange-looking old woman creating a ruckus at their private gate. Not André.

"I must talk to you," she said.

His expression became skeptical, but he took a few steps in her direction. "Yes?"

Her chest no longer pained her, and tears welled in her eyes at his kind words. Margaret must be proud of this man.

She, too, was proud. She had done the right

thing all those years ago, hadn't she? Was she doing the right thing now?

"I have something important to tell you." She steadied herself by grasping the fence. "About your mother."

He quickly opened the gate and came to her side. "What do you know about my mother? Where is she? Is she all right?"

He had grasped her hands in his. Wrenching anguish darkened his eyes. The tears that had pooled in Riva's eyes began to trickle down her lined cheeks.

"Please," he said.

Her silence was hurting him. She had to bring out the words.

"I don't know where Margaret is," she said, "but I knew her once, long ago. And I have something to tell you that she would want you to know, now that your family is in trouble."

ANDRÉ BROUGHT HER into the house. He couldn't quite decide why. That this woman with her colorful shabby clothing had ever known his mother seemed improbable. But there was something about her, something that touched him.

Margaret touched people's hearts that way, too.

This troubled old woman must be someone his mother had helped along the way, and now she wanted to share the story. André hadn't the heart to turn her away, although what he wanted more than anything was a quiet evening with his wife.

He wished for Gaby's presence right now; she was always so wise about how to handle difficult situations. She would know what to do. But his wife was upstairs with Andy-Paul and he hesitated to drag her into this and, in doing so, make more of it than it was.

Instead, he brought the old woman into the library. Her name, she said, was Riva Reynard Bechet.

André felt a moment of unease. Wasn't that the name of the woman who Scott said had some kind of fixation on the Lyon family? Then he recalled her tears. Perhaps her fixation was nothing more than gratitude for some long-forgotten helping hand.

Mrs. Bechet seemed to welcome the opportunity to sit. She closed her eyes for a moment, still clutching her outrageous purple shawl and the walking stick. He waited for her to speak.

"I knew your father first," she said at last, her voice thin and quavery. "Before he and Margaret married."

"You have a long history with my family, then," André said politely.

She was silent again for a while. When she spoke again, she looked him squarely in the eye. "There is no easy way. André, I am your mother."

André stood up abruptly. The old woman was senile. "I beg your pardon. Mrs. Bechet, this—"

"Please don't." Her voice was stronger now. "Paul and I, it meant nothing. But you were conceived. I didn't know that at first of course. By the time I knew, he was courting Margaret. I couldn't decide what to do. I was so afraid and I wanted what was best for you."

André felt light-headed. He needed Gaby. This whole story was absurd, an outrageous fabrication.

"Mrs. Bechet, if it's money you're after, I must tell you—"

She laughed, sadly, it seemed to him. "I want no money." She paused. "All I wanted was that my son have the best. That he not grow up a rich man's bastard. You see? So I talked to Margaret. I offered her my son. Her husband's son."

He felt short of breath. "I think it's best if you leave now."

The old woman continued as if he hadn't spoken. "To her credit, Margaret wanted the same thing. She wanted Paul's son to be raised as a Lyon. She is a remarkable woman, Margaret."

After all that had happened in court that morning, this woman's ridiculous story brought André to the breaking point. "I want you out of my home, Mrs. Bechet, now. And if you try to peddle your absurd lies anywhere else, I'll have you hauled into court for slander."

She stood, nodding. "I understand your feelings."

She walked toward the door. André trembled with the effort to remain standing until she was gone, and her ugly lies with her.

"You were named for my father," she said when she had her hand on the library door. "Margaret didn't mind. I don't think I've ever known a more selfless woman than her. To me, she is a saint."

Mrs. Bechet departed then. Left alone, André slumped into a chair, too drained for the moment even to climb the stairs in search of Gaby. The story was completely implausible of course. As unfounded as Alain's accusations.

But this woman's claim disturbed him as Alain's never had. This news, delivered by a frail

old woman with tears in her eyes, had shaken
him to the core.

Who was he? With both his parents now gone,
where could he turn for the answer?

CHAPTER FOURTEEN

RAYMOND THOUGHT he never would understand his older brother. Sometimes Alain reacted to things like an old woman.

One of these days he would find the gumption to say so to Alain's face, too.

They were in the private dining room at Chez Charles, having what should have been a celebratory dinner. The flinty-eyed judge—who had given Ray the creeps—had ruled in their favor. The other side of the family had been taken down a couple of notches; you could see that in the way they left the courtroom. Ray certainly thought raising a glass or two wasn't out of line.

But here sat Alain, his face as long as the last parade of Mardi Gras. Go figure.

"Move her," Alain said as he lit one of those Cuban cigars he liked to flaunt.

Raymond leaned across the table and spoke quietly. He was getting nervous about their little scheme these days. "Now? Why take a chance now?"

"You've got her too close. This trial will generate some news coverage. I don't want to run the risk that some bedpan jockey in backwater Arkansas will recognize her."

Raymond resisted the urge to roll his eyes. Alain thought he was the brains; Ray was beginning to think his brother was simply gutless. "Aw, come on, that's—"

"Move her."

The final word. The way it had always been. Well, Alain might not know it, but his days of giving orders were winding down. They were soon going to have more money and power than anyone else in the state. A fourth of it would belong to Ray, or a third of it if Scotty didn't wise up. Either way, whatever Alain had, Ray would have, too. Equals, that was what they'd be.

"Sure, sure. I'll take care of it."

"Immediately."

Jeez-Louise, sometimes Ray just wanted to take a pop at him. "You mean like now?"

"Yes, that's precisely what I mean."

Ray tossed his napkin onto the table and left Alain stinking up the private dining room with

his smelly cigar. To hell with what Alain wanted.
The old battle-ax was fine where she was.

SCOTT WAS EDITING tape for Nicki's video. He
liked the process. Enjoyed turning miles of ram-
bling seemingly unrelated film into a cohesive
view of some event or issue or person or place.

He rolled his shoulders and thought about calling it a day. He thought, too, about making calls
regarding a couple of jobs he'd heard about, but
he wasn't sure either was the sort of job he was
looking for. He wanted to do something satisfy-
ing, something rewarding. Maybe he should call
André, ask his opinion.

He began clearing away his work. Three days
had passed since the hearing. Since things with
Nicki had turned a corner. They hadn't made
love again, but Scott didn't need that to know
there was a greater intimacy between them. He
hadn't even seen her, but that was okay, too.
They had talked by phone—a lot. Maybe today
he would head out to Bayou Sans Fin.

Or maybe not. He didn't want to exert pressure
on Nicki.

He decided to phone WDIX-TV while he made
up his mind. First he would talk to André about
one of the jobs. André knew the people who ran

the company, could give him a rundown on them and whether they did work that mattered and not just work that made money.

But when the line was answered, André's secretary said his cousin wasn't in; when Scott asked when he might be able to catch André, Francie grew downright evasive and suggested he talk to Crystal. She transferred Scott to Crystal's line.

"What's going on, Crystal?" Scott asked as soon as she picked up. "Francie acted like a CIA agent when I asked for André."

There was a long silence. "I really don't appreciate having this dumped on me."

"Having what dumped on you?"

"If I thought for one minute that one of your brothers put you up to this..."

"What?"

"Okay, okay. I know better than that."

"So what gives? Is it about Aunt Margaret? You haven't found out something about Aunt Margaret, have you?"

"No. I wish I knew what it's about. Even Gaby doesn't seem to know. At least, she isn't saying."

Scott slumped in his chair. The family was disintegrating. "You're scaring me, Crystal."

"Sorry." She sighed deeply. "André hasn't been in since the hearing."

The announcement carried impact. Scott couldn't remember a single day when André hadn't been at the station. He even managed a few hours on days when no one else made an appearance—the day of his father's funeral, for example. That day he'd come in to oversee the handling of coverage of the funeral, to make sure the news department didn't go overboard. André had learned that kind of dedication from Margaret, he supposed. The station had been her baby for years, and now it was André's.

"I guess the ruling knocked him for a loop," he said.

"He seemed fine that afternoon. We all went for lunch and he was in pretty good spirits, confident things would work out in the end."

"So what happened?"

"Nobody knows. He didn't make it to dinner that night. Oh, God, Scott, Leslie said he hasn't been out of his room. We're all so worried. We've lost Uncle Paul and then Aunt Margaret, and I don't think the family can handle losing André, too."

Scott wished he could be there to put an arm around his cousin. "Give him time to regroup," he said, striving for a calm he really didn't feel. "He's had a lot of blows lately. It's understandable that he might need to…get away from things for a while."

"Right. And Aunt Margaret's on an island in the Caribbean, working through the stages of grief." Crystal sniffled. "Oh, great, and here I am crying. That's going to help a lot."

"How can I help?"

"I wish I knew. I keep thinking if we knew who he spoke to when he got home to Lyoncrest that afternoon, maybe we could figure out what's wrong with him. But he refuses to discuss it, Leslie said."

"He talked to someone? At the house?"

"Yes. Some crazy old woman. Nobody knew her, but André marched her right into the library and closed the door. She'd been banging on the fence, for heaven's sake—that's what the gardener said. Now that sounds odd, doesn't it?"

Scott's anxiety accelerated. "A crazy old woman?"

"She was wearing a hideous purple shawl of some kind. And walking with a cane. That's all the gardener could remember. And nobody in the family has any idea who she could be."

Scott murmured some comforting phrases, but

his mind was no longer on the conversation. His mind was on a crazy old lady with a purple shawl and a walking stick. He felt queasy. He wished for a moment that he'd never had the conversation with Crystal, that he could keep his head in the sand for just a bit longer.

But it wasn't going to be possible.

Whatever was going on between the Lyon family and the Bechet family, it was time to uncover it. The night Nicki had come to his house he'd had a feeling she knew something she wasn't telling him, and he'd ignored that feeling. No more. It was time to face whatever was coming.

Scott hated the thought of seeing fear and antagonism creep back into Nicki's face. He was afraid there wouldn't be enough magic to banish her demons twice.

Family. When was family going to stop ruining his life?

Nicki was beside herself.

Maman Riva had taken to her bed three days earlier. She refused to eat. She refused to see a doctor. She was weak and pale and the boundless spirit she'd had for as long as Nicki could remember seemed to have abandoned her. Nicki gazed at her grandmother, who lay against her pillow, eyes closed, so thin after just a few days that her body barely raised a bump under the sheets. Sighing, Nicki picked up the bowl of soup on the bedside table and leaned closer to her grandmother.

"Maman, you must eat," she said softly but insistently. "T-John made the soup. He said it's his best recipe."

The old woman made the faintest movement of her head. She hadn't spoken in days, either.

"Maman, don't do this," Nicki pleaded. She set the bowl of soup down again so she could brush away the tears gathering in her eyes. "Tell me what's wrong. I'll do anything. Whatever it is, I'll make it right. I promise. Please talk to me."

There was no reply, no reaction at all. For three days, none of her children, her grandchildren, or even her great-grandchildren, had been able to reach her. Like the stubborn old woman she was, Riva appeared to have made up her mind to die.

Nicki collapsed on the side of the bed, sobbing in frustration and anguish.

"Don't you die on me, Maman! Don't you dare!" she choked out.

She had almost exhausted her tears when she felt a hand on her shoulder. Expecting Michel or Beau or even Toni, she looked up into the troubled eyes of Scott. He gathered her into his arms and held her while she sobbed.

"You should have told me," he whispered. "I would have been here."

"I...I'm just not used to asking for help."

"Get used to it, Nicki."

She nodded, then pulled back to wipe her eyes and look at him. She was surprised to see him looking intently at her grandmother.

"How long has she been this way?"

Nicki worked to steady her voice. "Three days. Ever since she went out, Beau said. She came back and..." Nicki swallowed. "We thought maybe she'd done too much, that she just needed to rest. But she's...it's as if she's given up. As if she wants to die."

He looked at her then. "I love you, Nicki."

His timing struck her as odd, but at the moment she was so defenseless she had no choice but to say what she knew to be true. "And I love you, Scott. God knows, I love you."

"The last thing I want to do is hurt you," he said.

Again, his words seemed out of place. "I know that," she said.

"I need to talk to your grandmother. It might be best if you leave, but I think you'll want to stay."

"Of course I want to stay. Why wouldn't I? Scott, you're acting strange."

He kissed her then, very softly, and took her hand in his. He smiled, but it was a morose smile. Then he turned to speak to Riva.

"Mrs. Bechet, I know you aren't feeling well. You...might be interested in knowing that André isn't feeling well, either."

Nicki frowned. Why was he bringing up his cousin? She glanced at her grandmother and was surprised to see her eyelids flicker.

"What did you talk about, Mrs. Bechet? Why did you visit my cousin?"

How could he even think such a silly thing? "Scott, really..."

He held up a hand to silence her. "The gardener saw you. It *was* you, wasn't it, Riva?"

Nicki put a hand to her mouth, stifling a small cry. What could this mean?

"Riva, I love your granddaughter. I'd like to make a life with her and I think she's beginning to realize she could make a life with me, too."

He glanced at Nicki then, searching her face.
"But I'm afraid whatever is going on with your
family and mine, well, it's going to get in the
way of that. It's going to destroy our chances.

"André isn't talking, Riva. I think you're our
only chance. Nicki's only chance."

As urgently as Scott was pleading for revelation, Nicki felt the powerful urge to clamp a lid
on whatever lurked beneath the surface. Yes,
something she didn't understand had driven her
grandmother. Driven her to keep close tabs on
the Lyons for decades. Driven her to manipulate
their lives to bring the Lyons and the Bechets
together. Driven her to test the limits of her
eighty-four-year-old body in order to confront
one of those Lyons.

What secret bound Riva Bechet to the Lyon
family?

Nicki looked at Scott, then her grandmother,
and discovered the old woman studying her in
return. It was suddenly clear to Nicki that the
secret was killing Maman Riva.

She touched the old woman's cheek. It was
cool and surprisingly soft, despite the network of
fine lines that marked it. "Tell us, Maman."

Riva's bleary gaze traveled from Nicki's face
to Scott's, then back. Nicki saw a depth of love

and devotion in it that she had never seen before. Maybe her inability to see it before had been her own failing, rather than her grandmother's shortage of emotion. She had been so fearful of love, so unsure how to receive it, that she blocked it whenever it came her way.

She owed the change to Scott, to his gentle persistence.

She smiled at her grandmother and saw some of the worry in the old woman's face fade. Although the words came hard for Nicki, she knew what Riva needed to hear. "I love you, no matter what."

The snowy head moved in a slight nod. When she spoke, her voice was weak.

"In the drawer." She looked at Scott and gestured to her bedside table. "Take the picture."

Scott sent Nicki a questioning look. She shrugged, mystified. He opened the drawer and took out an old snapshot of her father, her uncle and her aunt. He studied it, then looked once again at Riva. "Yes?"

"My children," she said. "But one is missing." She looked at Scott. "André is your cousin." She turned to Nicki, "Your uncle." She closed her eyes. "My son."

Despite her assurances to her grandmother,

Nicki felt a moment of confusion, then denial, followed by a blast of anger. She wanted to back away, to guard herself against any consequences of her grandmother's admission. But she knew that was futile. The words were true. And they probably explained things Nicki had never fully understood.

Like the reason Maman Riva had sent her back to her father time after time, saying a child should not be separated from a parent. And the way her father had never felt he measured up in his mother's eyes.

Perhaps he hadn't. Perhaps he hadn't been imagining it at all. Perhaps Riva had always wished David were something more. Or someone else.

Riva told them the story in detail now, detail Nicki could barely absorb. The brief affair with Paul Lyon, the unorthodox deal struck with his young bride, and the bond that had developed between the two women over the years. The story was amazing and, to Nicki's mind, unquestionably true. She stared at her grandmother, and the unadorned truth blazed in the old woman's face. Riva Bechet would have done anything to protect that son, that first son, that lost son. And while she'd been raising the family not lost to her, a part of her had been far away, with the son she'd given up.

Nicki felt herself choking. She began to understand that her family would never be the same again. Her family would finally be swallowed by the Lyons.

CHAPTER FIFTEEN

THEY WALKED DOWNSTAIRS, not touching.

Scott wanted to touch Nicki, wanted to take her in his arms and comfort her. But he'd felt her withdrawal and wasn't sure he had the emotional energy to fight it. Not now. Not again. He was shell-shocked, too, drained by Riva Bechet's story.

He wanted to be there for Nicki. But this time he needed her to meet him halfway.

They reached the bottom of the stairs. She kept walking toward the front door.

"I guess this means I'm being escorted out again." He shoved his hands into his pockets to keep from grabbing her by the arm and forcing her to look him in the eye.

"Scott—"

"Out of the house. Out of your life." He knew he sounded bitter. She didn't deserve it, but he couldn't help it.

She turned on him. The tough Nicki faced him. "We can fight about this if you want to."

"Will it help you to blame me?"

"I'm not blaming you."

"My family, then?"

She flung open the front door. "I'm not blaming them for this...mess."

"Then what?"

She went out onto the porch and down the front steps. He followed her, remaining a few steps behind her as she headed for the water. He caught up with her at the old dock.

"Life is always messy, Nicki."

"Yes, it is."

"It's how we handle those messes that determines who we really are."

She wheeled on him. Her eyes were hard. "Save your little bits of wisdom, Scott. I'll handle it my way. And that may get messy, too."

"Fine."

He realized he was glaring at her, disappointment governing his reactions.

"What are you going to do with the information?" she asked.

Her question gave him a glimpse of the direction her fears were taking. Notoriety, scandal, the glare of the public eye all over again. He sympathized. But not enough to squelch his anger that the only way she could handle her fears was to turn on him.

"I don't know. I honestly don't know."

She gave him a skeptical look.

"I'd like us to be on the same side, Nicki. But we can't stand together if your first instinct is to turn against me every time the water gets rough."

He gave her a moment, hoping for some sign that she would take in his words and begin to come around. Her jaw twitched and her lips remained clamped tightly together. At last he turned and headed for his car, hoping he'd hear a sound from her, a movement in his direction. When he reached his car, he avoided looking toward the dock. He cranked up the volume on Merle Haggard and contemplated getting stinking drunk when he reached the city.

GETTING STINKING DRUNK took care of him for the rest of that evening. When he awoke the next morning, the problem of what to do still remained. Sitting on the side of his bed, he looked once again at the photograph Riva had given him. A hangover did not make it any easier to decide how to handle his family.

Or Nicki.

He wanted to call her, but he wouldn't. At least not yet.

First, he would go see Alain. Well, first he

would wait for his hangover to ease up. Then, he would go see his brother.

He made it to Alain's office by mid-afternoon, the distant drumbeat of a headache sounding in his right temple. If he avoided abrupt moves and loud noises, the drumbeat remained distant.

"You're looking a little ragged around the edges today, Scotty." Alain got up from his chair to pour a neat scotch at the bar to his left. He gestured questioningly at Scott, who shook his head. "Not hitting the sauce too much these days, are you? Being unemployed can do a number on a guy's head, you know. Leave him feeling emasculated."

Scott had heard that kind of dig from his brother for so long it took him a moment to recognize the sneer beneath it. He thought back to the way the Bechet cousins made playful verbal swipes at one another—no hostility hidden beneath those.

"I want you to drop the lawsuit," Scott said.

There. No game playing. A straight shot.

Alain paused with his glass halfway to his lips. His eyes narrowed almost imperceptibly. "You *must* be drinking."

"The whole thing is ludicrous and you know it. Not to mention demeaning to the family."

Alain set his glass on his desk with a firm

thunk. "What's demeaning is the way Paul and his side of the family have always slighted Dad and our side of the family."

"That's bunk and you know it."

Alain leaned across the desk, aiming for a little physical intimidation, Scott speculated. "Who have you been talking to? Somebody's been twisting your mind, little brother."

Scott stood, refusing to back down. "I've been listening to your sick thinking all my life and I'm fed up with it. Dad got less of the Lyon estate than Uncle Paul because he had no head for business. Then he managed to squander what he *had* been given. You know that as well as I do."

Alain pointed a finger at Scott's chest. "I'd keep Dad's shortcomings in mind if I were you. You haven't exactly proved yourself to be a go-getter, Scotty, and maybe you won't get your share once this is all settled."

"I don't give a damn about the family money, Alain. It's caused nothing but problems."

"You know, it's not a good strategy to make an enemy of me."

"Drop the lawsuit."

"Give me one good reason, aside from the fact that you're letting some of André's brood poison your mind."

"Because it's a damn lie. André is a Lyon and

you know it. Look at him. Listen to him. He's
Uncle Paul all over again.''

"You don't have all the facts.''

"No, *you* don't have all the facts.''

"Which are?''

Scott realized he'd gone too far. This wasn't
his information to share, especially with someone
as small-minded and devious as Alain. "Uncle
Paul is André's father. That's a fact, like it or
not.''

Alain picked up his scotch and took a lazy
swallow. "We have documents, you know. Hospital records. Adoption papers. That's going to
carry a lot more weight in a courtroom than anybody's opinion about family resemblance.''

"You're wrong, Alain. Don't do this.''

"I'm right. And you're wrong to cross me.''

"Think of something besides yourself for
once. Think of family.''

"Family! I am thinking of family. My family.
Our family. Not Aunt Margaret and that clan of
misfits she collected. You know this all goes
back to her. We have surgical reports showing
she couldn't conceive because of some kind of
infection when she was a kid. You didn't know
that, did you?''

No, he hadn't known that, and the satisfaction
on Alain's face revealed that he hadn't been able

to hide his surprise. That explained one more piece of the puzzling story Riva Bechet had narrated at Cachette en Bayou the day before. Aunt Margaret had been barren. But she had no doubt been determined to carry on the Lyon name in any way she could.

Riva Reynard Bechet had provided a way.

Alain smirked. "I thought not. Saint Margaret was pulling a fast one on all of us, Scotty. Dad always thought Margaret married Paul to snag a rich father for somebody else's kid. But the truth was a lot more devious than that. She duped the whole family. Isn't that rich?"

Scott wasn't sure he could listen much longer to something that was so far from the truth. "You're wrong, Alain. I want you to drop this business. Now."

"And if I don't?"

"I'll suggest to André that his private investigator find out why Raymond has been doing so much research into nursing homes lately. What do you think he'll learn, Alain?"

This time Alain's expression revealed that Scott had struck home.

Feeling slightly sick to his stomach and knowing it had nothing to do with his hangover, Scott left his brother's office.

SCOTT'S NEXT STOP was Lyoncrest.

He was told André wasn't accepting visitors. He walked upstairs, past the protesting house-keeper, past Gaby, who appeared at the top of the stairs and asked him to wait. He ignored her and sought out André's suite. He found his cousin sitting in an armchair beside a window overlooking the rose garden. André looked startled, then peeved, at the intrusion.

"Scott, if you don't mind, I've—"

"Just hear me out."

"Maybe later. I—"

Gaby burst into the room. "I'm sorry, dear. I tried to stop him, but—"

"I just came from Alain's. I told him to drop the suit. I don't know if he will, but if he doesn't, I'll tell him the truth. Then he'll have to stop."

André's expression closed. "I don't think you understand the ramifications of what you're saying." His tone was very measured.

Gaby walked over to André and stood behind him, a hand on his shoulder. She glared at Scott in a way he hoped never to see again. "Scott, aren't things in enough turmoil without stirring up more?"

Scott shook his head sadly. "No, Gaby. I've always been the one to keep quiet. Not anymore.'' He looked down at André. "I know about Riva Bechet.''

Gaby grew pale. André stared out the window. ''She's lying.''

"No, she isn't. And you know it. She has nothing to gain by lying.''

"Money,'' Gaby said. "Extortion. That's what I told André as soon as I heard about her outrageous claim.''

Scott fingered the photograph in his jacket pocket. "Did she threaten you, André? Ask for anything?''

"I didn't give her a chance.''

"I saw her yesterday. She's taken to her bed. Made up her mind to die.''

That apparently gave André pause. He made no comment. Gaby's shoulders seemed to collapse. "This is all so...inconceivable.''

Scott approached them and placed the photo into André's lap. "These are your brothers and your sister, André. Riva has letters, too, from Margaret.''

Gaby stifled a groan.

"My mother—''

"Your mother is lying in an old house on Bayou Sans Fin. All she wants is your forgiveness for doing what she believed was right for you.''

André didn't touch the photo in his lap. Gaby knelt by his side and clasped her husband's hands in hers. Struck by their devotion, Scott left. He supposed he'd managed to alienate both sides of his family now.

Well, he'd done what he'd had to.

If Aunt Margaret was here, she would understand.

NICKI TUCKED THE BLANKET around her grandmother's legs, taking a moment to appreciate the physical contact. The old woman muttered something as Nicki stepped back. How good it was to see Maman Riva sitting on the brick terrace, a little thinner, a little frailer, but enjoying the view of her domain once more.

Riva made a sound. "What was that?" Nicki asked.

Riva only grunted.

"I know you said something. What else can I do? More coffee?"

Perdu walked across Riva's shoulders to gaze at Nicki and pronounced, "Stop fussing."

Nicki laughed at the bird's perfect imitation of Riva's querulous tone. "You brought it on yourself," she retorted. "The next time you decide to take to your bed, be prepared to suffer the consequences."

Riva looked at her, a softness in her tired old eyes. "You're a good granddaughter, Nicolette."

Nicki dropped to her knees beside Riva and took one of the frail old hands in hers. "I'm working on it. And counting on you to hang around long enough to let me know when I make it."

Riva's eyes misted. She shook her head. "Might be I hang around too long already. Long enough to make a bad thing worse."

Nicki kissed her grandmother's knuckles. "Long enough to set things right."

"Ah, it is good Margaret is not here to see what this old fool has done."

"You loved her, didn't you?"

"She is a fine woman. The finest. I—" Riva cocked her head at the sound of a car door closing.

Nicki heard it, too, and her heartbeat picked up. They were expecting no one, although it might be Beau, who couldn't seem to get enough of his grandmother's company now that she had decided to rejoin the human race.

Or it might be Scott.

She took a moment to compose herself, then rose. "I'll see who it is."

Riva grasped her hand before she could move away. "Call him. I did not tell you all my secrets so you two could keep being foolish. You do this.''

''Maman—''

Perdu squawked, ''Call. Foolish. Foolish.''

Someone was now knocking on the front door; it definitely wasn't Beau. ''I'll think about it, Maman.''

Riva grunted again; Perdu screeched.

Nicki couldn't squelch her excitement as she opened the door. It was time to tell Scott she was ready to face the future with him. The words trembled on her lips, ready to flow forth.

It was André Lyon, looking unsure of himself.

''Mr. Lyon!''

He cleared his throat. ''You're Scott's friend. I, uh, I wondered if... I know I've intruded. But I was hoping to speak with Mrs. Bechet.''

She studied his face. This was Maman's son. Once again she noted the similarities in carriage between her father and this man, the easy looseness, counterbalanced by the way they tucked their hands into their trouser pockets. She recognized the way he rolled his shoulders beneath his suit, a habit of her father's when he was faced with something unpleasant.

The hairs stood up on the back of her neck.

She wanted to deny him access to her grandmother simply because he was so much like her father.

But André Lyon wasn't to blame for that.

She stepped back and opened the door to admit him. As he followed her down the hall toward the back of the house, she felt compelled to speak. "She's eighty-four. She hasn't been well."

He met her eyes. "I understand."

"If she doesn't want to see you..."

"I won't press her."

Nicki let out her breath. "Thank you."

She pointed to the door leading to the back terrace. Although there was no reason to, she trusted him with her grandmother. She thought of Scott. Maybe that was the similarity between the two men, an innate gentleness that inspired trust.

She went back to her office, unsure she could concentrate. But she had barely settled in her chair when her own problems absorbed her.

The list was lying on her keyboard, where she'd dropped it as soon as it printed out. Four nursing homes, all within a few hours of New Orleans. All with residents who could be Margaret Lyon, based on a number of details, including dates of arrival and similarity of names.

One of which also employed a nurse's aide by the name of Debra B. Minor.

She stared at the list, weighing her options. She measured her courage against her cowardice.

How many Debra B. Minors could there be? This one at Whispering Pines Nursing Facility in Arkansas had to be the woman who had given birth to a six-pound, twelve-ounce baby girl in New Orleans, Louisiana, on April 21, 1964.

What if Debra B. Minor didn't want to be found by the daughter she had left behind?

Nicki felt the scales tip in favor of cowardice. After all, she already had one confrontation to face. One was plenty.

She picked up the phone and dialed, holding her breath, hoping Scott answered because she wasn't sure she could find the courage to make the call a second time. After the fourth ring, his voice brought to life every nerve ending in her body. "Scott here."

"It's me."

"Nicki."

He said her name tentatively. She'd hoped for welcome in his voice. She couldn't blame him for reserving judgment.

"I…" *I miss you. I want a second chance. I want as many chances as you'll give me to make it right.* "André is here."

A brief silence. "That's good."

She should have felt calmer; this was safer ground. She didn't. "They'll work it out."

"I hope so."

"You talked to him," she said.

Another silence. Getting involved in family affairs was something Scott had always avoided, he'd told her. Obviously, however, he'd found a way to go against the grain.

Courage.

She took a deep breath. "There's a woman at a nursing home I'd like us to visit."

"Where?"

"Whispering Pines, Arkansas. She's registered as Mrs. Margie Paul."

"Do you think…?"

"It could be nothing. I just figured the name was quite a coincidence."

"When can we go?"

"Scott, I—"

"I'll be there in an hour."

She opened her mouth to protest, but he'd already hung up. "I can't," she whispered to the empty room.

But she would. She knew that. When Scott came for her, she would go.

CHAPTER SIXTEEN

ANDRÉ SAT IN THE CHAIR across from the woman who claimed to be his birth mother. He still didn't want to accept it. Just being here he felt disloyal to the woman he'd always called Mother, a woman who wasn't here to explain her side of things.

But André had never been a man to shy away from harsh reality. And if Riva Reynard Bechet was indeed his mother, he didn't want to wake up one morning and realize he'd let the chance to know her slip through his fingers. Gaby had helped him see that. As had the photograph Scott gave him.

Was it possible, at his age, that he was going to discover the brothers and sisters he'd always wanted? That thought—and the subsequent one of all the lost years—was a sharp ache.

He looked at the woman and said weakly, "I'm ready to listen."

"And I am ready to talk. As ready as I shall ever be."

She began to rock. Her eyes closed. Her voice grew so soft he had to strain to hear.

"She was very young, Margaret was. Much younger than I was. Not just in years, either, you understand. Eighteen and just married."

He tried to picture his mother—Margaret—being that young, but it wasn't easy.

"I was desperate. I had no way to care for you. My family would have disowned me. In those days, it was different. And a woman alone..." She shook her head. "I wanted more than that for you. I wanted you to grow up the way you deserved. With your father. With all the privilege and opportunity he could provide. Things I couldn't provide. So I went to see Margaret."

André had a million questions. And his feelings about this frail and weathered-looking woman who claimed to have given birth to him were shifting. Her story was so poignant. And if it was true... My God, if it was true...

"I don't know why she agreed, except that she had a heart so big it had room for the son of the man she loved." She stroked the cat in her lap. "We made a vow. It would be our secret. And Paul's, too, of course." She smiled. "Although Paul was too stubborn to listen to the truth for years."

André remembered the years of his father's absence and the way it had been explained. The possibility that there was another explanation for that absence knocked the breath out of him.

Riva Bechet continued. "Margaret always kept her vow. And now I have broken mine."

"Why? Why now?"

"Maybe because of this problem with Charles and his sons. Maybe because of Scott and Nicki. They are in love, those two. They are caught in the middle. Or maybe just because of Margaret. With her gone, I... Maybe I am selfish. I needed someone else to know. I needed not to carry this secret to my grave."

As Margaret had—that was her implication.

He stared at Riva Bechet, taking in every detail of her appearance. He tried to imagine his father with her, but the image was impossible. His father had loved Margaret with every beat of his heart, every breath he drew. Of that there could be no question. But something about the simplicity of what Riva Bechet said had convinced André.

Actually he'd been convinced from the moment he'd looked at that photograph. "Tell me about when I was born," he said.

And she did.

All the details she recounted fit perfectly with the details Margaret had told him countless times when he was a child. Only the identity of the birth mother changed. Thinking of the tenderness with which Margaret had shared the story of his birth—and knowing now what it must have cost her—tore at his heart.

Had a child ever been more loved? By both women who had mothered him?

When she finished the story, Riva Bechet had tears running down her cheeks. He had the impulse to go to her and put his arm around her, but he wasn't quite ready to do that yet. Maybe someday.

They talked for three hours. He was aware, as the time passed, that someone else came into the house, then left. But no one interrupted their meeting on the shady brick terrace.

When he rose to leave, she took one of his hands in hers. "I want you to know something very important. I gave birth to you. But the woman who made you into the man you are today, the woman who was your real mother in every way that mattered, this was Margaret."

He left quickly then, before he, too, had tears in his eyes.

THE OLD WOMAN in room 19 was dying. Debra Minor had enough nurse's training under her belt to know that. In fact, a less determined person would have been dead long ago. But Mrs. Paul, even in the physical and mental state she was in, had more strength of will than anyone Debra had ever met.

"That's why it breaks my heart to see you like this, Mrs. Paul," she whispered, gently brushing with her fingertips the place where the IV needle pierced the woman's fragile skin. She would have liked to smooth away the ugly purple bruise. "That's why it makes me so goldarned mad when nobody here will listen to me. I tell 'em and tell 'em you're on too much medication, but nobody pays me any mind."

She looked over her shoulder as she said it, to make sure the door to the corridor was still closed.

"And that's why I'm so worried about this relative of yours they said is on the way. Mr. Raymond. They said the orders come from some doctor. But I don't trust Mr. Raymond or his doctor, either. You like Mr. Raymond, Mrs. Paul?"

There was no response. She hadn't expected one.

"I didn't think so. He wants to take you to another nursing home. Today."

Debra's rage mounted as she thought about it. "Now, I know darn well there are better places for you to be. But the truth is, you're in no condition to be moved right now.''

A part of her wanted to take Mrs. Paul home with her, where the poor woman could at least die in peace.

Debra thought about that. About unhooking every blessed one of these IVs and all the other contraptions and wheeling Mrs. Paul right out the back door. She'd never make it of course. And she'd lose her job. Maybe even wind up in prison if—when—Mrs. Paul died.

She thought for a moment what it would be like when she was this age, with nobody to watch out for her. She thought about it long and hard. While she was thinking, she unhooked the IV. She kept talking to the old woman in a soft reassuring murmur. She told herself if she was going to do this, she needed a plan, and she didn't have one. This was pure insanity.

At least if they called the police, maybe someone would sit up and take notice of Mrs. Paul. If that happened, it would be worth it.

THEY WERE TOO EDGY to do much talking in the first half hour of their trip as they sped toward Whispering Pines, Arkansas. They had greeted each other awkwardly, then got into Scott's sports car without touching.

Nicki had wanted to throw her arms around him. She had longed for a few simple words that would set right all that was unsettled between them. But it would take more than a few words, she supposed. And more important issues needed their attention at the moment.

"What are you thinking about?" she finally asked.

She thought for a moment he wasn't going to answer.

"Aunt Margaret."

She nodded. There was no reason to feel disappointed.

"You?" he asked.

She pondered which part of her obsessive thinking to reveal to him. It occurred to her that his long pause before his last reply might have reflected the same sorting through options.

"My mother."

"Your mother?"

She nodded, then remembered he was facing the road. "There's a nurse's aide at this home. Her name is Debra Minor. Debra B. Minor."

He let out a low whistle. "Wow."

"Of course, it may not be her."

"There's a good chance."

"Yes." She realized her fists were clinched in her lap and forced herself to relax, spreading her fingers, opening her palms. "I was wondering what she looks like. Whether she has gray hair now. If..."

She stopped herself.

He reached over and took one of her hands in his. "She'll be glad to see you."

The touch and the way he read her mind undid her. She pressed her free hand to her eyes. "I hope so."

He held her steady with one hand, the car with his other hand. The countryside whizzed past. Nicki closed her eyes and tried to relax. But more thoughts kept spinning to the surface, demanding release.

"And you. Us. I was thinking about us."

Her mouth went dry waiting for him to reply.

"Were you?"

"Yes. That I was glad we were in this together. And..."

He gave her hand a squeeze. "And what?"

"And I'd like to give us another chance."

"Why?"

"Because I love you. And I hope you still love me."

She waited for him to answer. He was holding her hand. That meant something, didn't it?

"I'm not sure that's enough," he said. She heard the regret in his voice, but the message still hurt. Before she could respond, she spotted the turnoff to Whispering Pines. Grateful for the distraction, she reached for her canvas bag and the map she'd marked to guide them to the nursing home.

"Look," she said briskly, all business. "We're almost there. Left here, then three miles to Old Church Road, then right to the nursing home."

He followed her directions. Five minutes later they spotted the cinderblock nursing home, surrounded by a barren asphalt parking lot and a few scraggly pines. Scott braked to a halt behind another car with a Louisiana license plate.

"That's my brother's car," he said grimly.

Scott bounded out of the car without waiting for her. She followed at a trot, her heart heavy with dread. By the time she reached the reception area, Scott was already engaged in a shouting match with a woman in a pale green uniform.

"Tell me, or I'll tear this place apart! Then I'll have you up on charges for accessory to kidnapping!"

The woman's eyes grew large. "Why, I—"

A younger woman behind her said, "Room 19. That way."

Scott took off in the direction the woman indicated, and Nicki followed, but not without a backward glance at the woman behind the desk. Could she be Debra Minor?

She stared at every woman in uniform she passed, searching for name tags. She felt equal measures of disappointment and relief each time she didn't see the name Debra Minor.

She reached room 19. The door stood open. She peered in just in time to see Scott take a swing at the other man in the room. His fist connected, sending the well-dressed man flailing against a rolling metal bed tray. He landed in a heap against a wall, groaning, rubbing his jaw.

Scott gathered the frail old woman in the bed into his arms and held her against his chest. Tears glistened on his eyelashes and he murmured over and over again, "Aunt Margaret, Aunt Margaret, I'm here. Everything's going to be all right now. You just hang on. You hear me? Just hang on."

Nicki's heart swelled as she looked at him, holding the old woman with the protectiveness of a man who could be depended on. She walked over to him and lightly kissed his forehead, then sat beside him with her hand on his shoulder.

She didn't know if he even registered her presence, but it didn't matter. She would go to him again later. And she would tell him that she loved him and was ready to trust him completely. That finally she understood that love and commitment

were two sides of the same coin. Her heart felt
suddenly and overwhelmingly ready to burst with
emotions that she had denied herself for so long.
As she sat there, at once both content to simply
be close to him and impatient to tell him how she
felt, she heard a rustling behind her. She glanced
over her shoulder and saw a woman in uniform
leaning against the wall, hand over her heart and
tears rolling down her cheeks. Embroidered on
her chest in crisp white script was her name.

Debra.

IT TOOK SOME TIME to straighten everything out.

Nicki watched intently from the sidelines as
Scott spoke to the nursing-home management,
then to police, then to some other law-
enforcement people in suits. The men in suits
took Raymond with them. An ambulance came
for Margaret.

Through it all, Nicki kept an eye on Debra,
who also stood by on the fringes, her attention
focused completely on Margaret Lyon. More
than once, Debra made a motion in the old
woman's direction, a proprietary move that said
she was having a hard time trusting the patient's
care to someone else.

When Scott went with Margaret while they
wheeled her to the waiting ambulance, Nicki ap-

proached the nurse's aide. The woman seemed nervous.

"I'm sorry about Mrs. Paul—I mean, Mrs. Lyon. I kept telling 'em something wasn't right. But nobody listens to an aide." She backhanded a tear. "Lord have mercy, that poor woman. I'm so sorry."

She spoke in a slow drawl, very different from the cadence of speech Nicki was accustomed to on the bayou. From somewhere deep in her memory she heard her father saying Debra's voice was like pouring sugarcane syrup on a January morning.

Nicki drew a deep breath. "My name is Nicolette. Nicolette Bechet."

It took a moment, apparently, for her words to sink in. Then Debra gasped and her eyes grew wide.

"Are you," Nicki asked haltingly, "my... mother?"

A sob was torn from Debra's lips. "Nicki? My baby?"

Every bit of control Nicki had so carefully hoarded during her life broke loose.

The two women fell into each other's arms.

SCOTT CAME BACK into the reception area, the whine of the ambulance fading in the distance.

His head was spinning. There was so much to be
done. He had called Lyoncrest almost immediately of course. The family would arrive within
the hour at the local hospital where Margaret was
being taken. Scott wanted to be there. For once,
he wanted to be caught up in the circle of his
family's love.

And he wanted to take Nicki with him.

The most distinct memory he had from the past
two hours was sitting on that hospital bed, Aunt
Margaret limp and barely breathing in his arms,
and feeling Nicki's touch. He was through holding back, and the tenderness in her touch told him
she was, too. Impatient to see her, he rushed to
room 19 and found her wrapped in the embrace
of the nurse's aide who had probably saved Margaret's life. The aide's name, he knew, was Debra Minor.

As anxious as he was to get to the hospital, he
waited by the door. He watched mother and
daughter hug and cry and talk. His emotions were
so close to the surface it was all he could do not
to cry himself. In fact, he had looked away to
compose himself when he felt Nicki's hand on
his shoulder. He turned; he thought her tear-
streaked face had never been more beautiful.

"Oh, Scott." Her voice broke when she spoke.

He took her in his arms and she clung to him.

Over her shoulder, he could see her mother, sitting on the recently vacated bed, a worried and loving gaze lingering on her daughter. Scott felt the tears he'd barely managed to contain collect in the corners of his eyes.

Nicki murmured against his shoulder, "It's all too much to take in."

"I know."

"But it's going to work out."

"I know."

"She has a picture of me. In her wallet. When I was three. She showed me."

As he heard the childlike hope in her voice, Scott also felt his love for her well up in his chest, filling him with too many emotions to name. He felt relief and gratitude that she had been given the gift of finding her mother's love again. She had craved it for so long, just as he had craved family.

They were kindred spirits, more than either of them had realized. "That's good, Nicki. Very good."

"She said...said she was too young to know what she was doing." Her eyes filled. "She said Dad, my dad, was so much like her father it scared her. The way he drank, you know. She said she knew she was too young to take care of me herself and thought Dad would go back to the farm. She knew I'd be fine there with my grand-mother to watch out for me.'' She pulled away to get a tissue from her pocket and took a swipe at her eyes. ''Oh, Scott, she meant to do the right thing for me. Just the way Maman Riva was try-ing to do the right thing for André. It's just like you said. Life is full of messes.''

''Yes, it is.''

''But she said she loved me. She's...she's coming home with me.''

''That's wonderful, sweetheart. I'm very happy for you.''

She leaned against him and he wrapped his arms around her again.

''Scott?''

''Yes, Nicki.''

''I love you.''

''And I love you,'' he said.

She sighed softly. ''Do you?''

''How could I not?''

''I...I've never been sure I'm all that lov-able.''

He saw the remnants of self-doubt in her eyes. He bent over her to kiss each eyelid, wishing the touch of his lips could banish those feelings for-ever. He knew it would take time and he was ready to devote his life to the task. ''Oh, but you are,'' he said. ''I'll show you. Today and tomorrow and every day.''

She smiled. ''Every day?''

''I promise.''

''And we won't walk away. Not even when the going gets tough.''

He touched a wild curl that curved against her cheek. ''We'll have the best knock-down, dragout fights Cachette en Bayou's ever seen. But no walking away.''

She closed her eyes and laughed. He took the opportunity to kiss her.

Thirty minutes later, when they walked into the hospital where his family had assembled, they walked together.

EPILOGUE

Two months later

MARGARET LYON mustered every bit of strength and courage she had to approach the lectern and face the swarm of cameras and microphones.

Everyone was here to see her, to make sure the stories of her return were true. She had been determined to face them as soon as possible—despite her doctor's recommendation that she wait another few weeks—and under her own power. She had rejected out of hand the idea of a wheelchair, a walker or a cane.

She even refused André's offer to escort her to the lectern.

Her head held high, she stepped up to the microphone and smiled at the media. Ah, it was good to be home, in the thick of things.

It was good to be alive.

"I know you're all here today to see how the old broad looks after her ordeal," she said in a strong voice.

Laughter greeted her.

"Well, I won't hazard a guess as to how the old broad looks, but she feels great."

More laughter. Even from behind her on the stage, Margaret could pick out the laughter of those she loved. André and Gaby, her granddaughter Leslie and her husband Michael, even Crystal and her husband Caleb. Only Charlotte was missing, but her youngest granddaughter's pregnancy had made the trip from San Francisco impossible.

But there was Riva. It was good to have Riva with her. It felt right.

"But I'm not here to talk about all that juicy family gossip you're dying for me to get to," she continued. Not that the family had tried to hide any of it. Margaret had been adamant. She was through with hiding behind white lies, through with worrying what the rest of the world thought about the Lyon family.

"I am here today to launch a new venture— the Lyon-Bechet Foundation." She paused. She was tiring quickly. No matter, she would turn this over to a new generation in a matter of seconds. "Established solely with family financing, the Lyon-Bechet Foundation will assist in the location of missing persons."

She took some satisfaction in the murmur that went through the crowd.

"As you all know, we've had some hands-on experience in that area. And most of the credit for that goes to the two people who will head the foundation—my nephew Prescott Lyon and his wife, Nicolette Bechet Lyon. They're both much more photogenic than I am, so you'll be pleased to hear that I will now turn the floor over to them for your questions."

She paused to share a hug with Scott and Nicki as they approached the lectern. They had married quickly and quietly, in a small ceremony at Lyoncrest, while Margaret was still recovering. Then she'd had the chance to get to know Nicki better as the three of them made plans for the foundation. Margaret had long loved Scott for his gentle spirit, which was perfectly complemented, in her opinion, by Nicki's prickly energy. They were good for each other.

And they were supremely happy. Margaret knew love when she saw it and this was it.

She sat between Riva and André and let her mind wander as the newlyweds responded to questions. She couldn't remember ever having been so satisfied. All her life, it seemed, she had been striving for one more success, one more accomplishment, one more way to fulfill the Lyon legacy. All the accomplishments had been good. But the things that had come out of this latest crisis, they were the legacy she'd always wanted deep in her heart.

For with her here on stage today was not only Riva and her clan, but Charles's boys, as well. Charles was too ill to be with them, but Jason was here with his family, a fine young bunch she looked forward to knowing better. Alain and Raymond were here, too, with their families. And for the first time in their lives, Margaret believed, Alain and Raymond were coming to accept their role in the family. They had been humbled by their experience, and dumbfounded by Margaret's efforts to have the charges against them reduced and their sentence set at probation.

For the first time in their lives, she believed, they truly understood what she meant when she told them, "Family comes first."

And there was Debra Minor of course. Margaret's gratitude to the woman who'd saved her life knew no bounds. Debra had been invited to join them on the stage, but had declined. She was still getting used to the family she had suddenly inherited. Margaret smiled. Everyone adored Debra, who had settled in happily at Cachette en Bayou.

Riva leaned closer and whispered, "I'm only sorry Paul isn't here to see this."

Margaret, too, had been thinking of Paul. But she knew with certainty that the man she loved was looking on as she finally created the perfect Lyon legacy—a strong and harmonious family. She smiled at her friend, discreetly touched her heart and said, "Oh, but he is."

If you missed any of the previous
LYON LEGACY *books,*
you can order them from
Harlequin Reader Service
U.S.: 3010 Walden Ave., P.O. Box 1325,
Buffalo, NY 14269
Canada: P.O. Box 609,
Fort Erie, Ont. L2A 5X3

#847 THE LYON LEGACY,
Peg Sutherland, Roz Denny Fox,
Ruth Jean Dale

#853 FAMILY SECRETS,
Ruth Jean Dale

#859 FAMILY FORTUNE,
Roz Denny Fox

#865 FAMILY REUNION,
Peg Sutherland

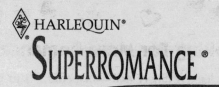

HARLEQUIN®
SUPERROMANCE®

Join us in celebrating Harlequin's 50th Anniversary!

The *LYON LEGACY* is a very special book containing *three* brand-new stories by three popular Superromance® authors, Peg Sutherland, Roz Denny Fox and Ruth Jean Dale—all in one volume!

In July 1999, follow the fortunes of the powerful Lyon family of New Orleans. Share the lives, loves, feuds and triumphs of three generations... culminating in a 50th anniversary celebration of the family business!

The Lyon Legacy continues with three more brand-new, full-length books:

August 1999—**FAMILY SECRETS** by Ruth Jean Dale
September 1999—**FAMILY FORTUNE** by Roz Denny Fox
October 1999—**FAMILY REUNION** by Peg Sutherland

Available wherever Harlequin books are sold.

HARLEQUIN®
Makes any time special ™

Looking For More Romance?

Visit Romance.net

Check in daily for these and other exciting features:

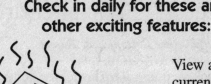

Hot off the press

View all current titles, and purchase them on-line.

What do the stars have in store for you?

Horoscope

Hot deals

Exclusive offers available only at Romance.net

Plus, don't miss our interactive quizzes, contests and bonus gifts.

PWEB

HARLEQUIN®
Makes any time special ™

In celebration of Harlequin®'s golden anniversary

Enter to win a *dream!* You could win:

- A luxurious trip for two to *The Renaissance Cottonwoods Resort* in Scottsdale, Arizona, or
- A bouquet of flowers once a week for a year from **FTD**, or
- A $500 shopping spree, or
- A fabulous bath & body gift basket, including **K-tel**'s *Candlelight and Romance* 5-CD set.

Look for **WIN A DREAM** flash on specially marked Harlequin® titles by Penny Jordan, Dallas Schulze, Anne Stuart and Kristine Rolofson in October 1999*.

RENAISSANCE.
COTTONWOODS RESORT
SCOTTSDALE, ARIZONA

K·TEL

"This book is DYNAMITE!"
—**Kristine Rolofson**

"A riveting page turner…"
—**Joan Elliott Pickart**

"Enough twists and turns to keep everyone
guessing… What a ride!"
—**Jule McBride**

See what all your favorite authors
are talking about.

Coming October 1999 to a retail store near you.

HARLEQUIN®
SUPERROMANCE®

by
Janice Kay Johnson

The people of Elk Springs, Oregon, thought
Ed Patton was a good man, a good cop,
a good father. But his daughters know the truth....

Renee, Meg, Abby
Sisters, Cops...Women

They're not like their father. And that's all right with them. But
they still feel they have something to prove to the
townspeople—and to themselves.

Daniel, Scott, Ben—three men who can see past the
uniforms to the women inside. They're willing to
take on—and ready to love—Patton's Daughters.

Look for Janice Kay Johnson's newest miniseries:

August 1999—*The Woman in Blue* (#854)
September 1999—*The Baby and the Badge* (#860)
October 1999—*A Message for Abby* (#866)

Available at your favorite retail outlet.

HARLEQUIN®
Makes any time special ™